Hometown Proposal
Merrillee Whren

Steeple
Hill®

Published by Steeple Hill Books™

STEEPLE HILL BOOKS

Steeple
Hill®

Recycling programs
for this product may
not exist in your area.

ISBN-13: 978-0-373-87615-0

HOMETOWN PROPOSAL

Copyright © 2010 by Merrillee Whren

www.SteepleHill.com

Printed in U.S.A.

Blessed are the merciful, for they will be shown mercy.

—*Matthew* 5:7

I would like to dedicate this book to my daughter
Danielle, who is my first reader,
and her husband, Paul.

Acknowledgments
I want to thank Rachel Daubenmire for giving me
information about physical therapy.
All mistakes are mine.

Chapter One

"Juliane, tell me you're not serious. Tell me Seth Finlay is *not* joining us for dinner tonight." Staring across the kitchen table at her sister, Juliane, Elise Keller gripped the top of the Windsor back chair until her knuckles turned white. She gritted her teeth as a crushing sensation took her breath away.

"I'm sorry, Elise, but it's true. He'll be meeting us at Mom and Dad's."

Elise counted to ten with the hope that her words would come out in a calm cadence rather than in a shriek. "How could Dad have invited Seth? For that matter, how could he have hired him in the first place? What was he thinking?"

Juliane, dressed in the navy blue suit she'd worn to work, took a step back. "We've been over this. Dad didn't do the hiring. Nathan did. Dad was only on the committee. And just like he told you, he thought Seth was the best man for the job, along with all the other committee members. After all, his experience as a cruise director makes him very qualified to run the new recreation facility. Even you had to admit he was good at his job. And since you won't talk about the problems you two had other than to say they were personal and not job related, the committee made the only logical choice."

Taking a deep breath, Elise closed her eyes. Seth's image clouded her thoughts. She tried to shake away the image of his handsome face with the chiseled cleft chin, but his tall, lean physique marched through her mind and left a snapshot. His dark brown eyes, which matched his hair, seemed to stare at her from the back of her brain. "That still doesn't explain why we're having dinner with him tonight."

"I don't know. Maybe you can ask Dad tonight."

Elise narrowed her gaze. "And no one was going to tell me that Seth is going to be there?"

"That was the plan. Mom and Dad have no idea what went wrong with the two of you. I think they're hoping you'll work things out now that Seth is in town. But nothing can happen if you won't see him, which is why they didn't tell you. But I thought you deserved to know."

Elise released a heavy sigh. "I don't believe this."

"Well, believe it."

Crossing her arms at her waist, Elise shook her head. "How am I going to handle this?"

Scrunching up her face, Juliane hunched her shoulders. "I don't have a clue."

"Great." Elise clenched her fists, trying to fight back the fury. "I've been ignoring his attempts to contact me for over a year. Now not only is he moving to town, but I have to have dinner with him tonight. Did you just find out about this today, too?"

Juliane lowered her gaze.

"You knew about this and didn't tell me, didn't you?" Fists still clenched, Elise raised her arms and beat at the air. "How could you keep the information from me until the last minute?"

"I'm sorry." Juliane let out a harsh breath. "I just thought you needed some closure with this guy. Rid yourself of the bad feelings. It's not healthy to carry around the anger or whatever it is you feel toward him. You know from my experience that forgiveness is a great healer."

Trying to relax, Elise took a deep breath and dropped her hands to her sides. Juliane was right, but Elise didn't want to talk about forgiveness. "I had closure with Seth when I quit my job on the cruise ship and came home to get away from him. I don't need him coming around and dredging up the past."

"It's been over a year since you moved back to Kellerville, and I think you're still not over the past. You've been running away from it ever since you returned."

"What makes you say that?"

"You won't talk about what happened between you and Seth."

"What good would that do?" Shaking her head, Elise wished Juliane could let it go. "Seeing him won't help get rid of anything. I just want to forget."

"But you're not forgetting, are you? Be honest."

Crossing her arms again, Elise pressed her lips together. She didn't want to admit that her sister was right. "Okay. I haven't forgotten, but seeing Seth Finley again promises turmoil in my life. Everything is going so well. Why would I want to throw Seth into the mix? It would be like frosting a cake with mud."

"That's an unappealing analogy." Juliane laughed half-heartedly. "There's nothing you can do about it. Seth's here whether you like it or not."

"Thanks for the encouragement." Elise couldn't keep the sarcasm out of her voice.

Juliane walked around the table and put a hand on Elise's arm. "Hey, sis, I know you're not happy about this, but you can deal with it. You're a strong woman."

"Well, this strong woman has to study, then figure out how to be pleasant to Seth Finley. Let me know when you're ready to head for Mom and Dad's." Elise rushed from the kitchen before Juliane could give her any more advice or bad news.

Elise took the stairs to her second-floor bedroom two at a time as if she were trying to outrun the images of Seth that still floated through her mind. Sitting at her desk, she opened her textbook. As she tried to study, the words swam in her head along with memories she couldn't shake.

Concentration wouldn't come.

Was she strong, as Juliane had said? She didn't feel that way. When Seth had called several months after she'd returned to her little hometown in southwestern Ohio, she'd refused to talk to him, hanging up as soon as she'd heard his voice. Now she feared how she'd handle all her unresolved feelings.

She'd spent the past eighteen months pushing thoughts of him further and further to the back of her mind until she'd convinced herself that they were locked in a dark corner never to resurface. But the prospect of his appearing had unlocked the door and let the memories run wild.

She had loved him—but he'd broken her heart when he'd proven just how far he was from the honorable man she'd believed him to be. She should have known better. He'd led her far away from the principles she'd learned growing up. Nothing good could come from seeing that man.

She worried that Seth's presence in this town would throw her life off course. Despite her ill will toward him, her feelings were still so confused. How much of their relationship had been as real for him as it had been for her? She couldn't be sure. She wanted answers, but was afraid of them at the same time.

Light tapping sounded on the door. Time to go already? Elise jumped out of her chair. Before she reached the door, Juliane stepped into the room. Gazing at her diminutive sister, Elise straightened to her nearly six-foot height, a great intimidator. "I suppose this means it's time to go."

Juliane sighed. "Don't act like you're going to your execution. I came up to tell you that we'll be leaving in half an hour."

"Thanks for the warning. Am I dressed appropriately for the evening?" Holding out her arms, Elise twirled around.

"That's up to you. I'm wearing what I've got on. If you want to wear your jeans, that's your choice." Juliane raised an eyebrow. "Worried about what Seth will think?"

"No. What Dad will say."

"It's your call. Thirty minutes."

As Juliane left the room, Elise looked out the window at the backyard below. Lilies of the valley displayed their little white blossoms in a shady corner of the yard. Springtime brought with it the hope for warmer weather, but there was no way she could feel any hope about seeing Seth Finley again. She vowed not to let him mess up her life once more.

When she first met him, she was a college dropout who'd fled home with a job singing on a cruise ship. After the strain of hiding her father's alcoholism, she'd needed to get away. But those years had led her away from her family and God, making it hard to come home. Now, seven years later, she was back home, and her life was coming together. Finally, her dad had acknowledged his drinking problem and was getting help.

Since her return a year and a half before, she'd gone back to college while working part-time at her family's department store. She'd reconciled with her family and with God. At the end of the summer, she expected to finish her courses and get her music education degree. Life was good.

Under no circumstances was she going to let Seth's appearance derail her plans.

Seth stopped his car in the driveway of Ray Keller's red-brick ranch house just outside of Kellerville. Turning, Seth looked at his two-and-a-half-year-old daughter. "Olivia, we're here."

"Daddy, get me out." She worked to undo the buckle.

"I'll let you out in a minute." Seth opened the back door and released Olivia from the car seat. "Okay, you have to be a good girl tonight and do what Daddy says."

"'Kay." Nodding, Olivia wrapped her little arms around his neck as he lifted her out of the car. Seconds later, she squirmed to get down. "Me get down."

As Seth set her down, she wiggled out of his grasp. Dark curls bobbing, she scampered up the walk toward the front door. With the distraction of a cute toddler, dressed in a pink sweater and pink pants covered in little flowers, he couldn't concentrate on the impending encounter with Elise. He only had time to think about the little girl whose favorite color was pink, even though she lived with a single dad.

Grinning, Seth hurried after her and swung her up into his arms. "Whoa there!"

She giggled. The sound touched him deep inside as he gathered her close. He loved this child more than he'd ever thought possible, in spite of all the problems she'd caused. She'd turned his world upside down and inside out. Her presence was a huge hurdle that he would have to overcome in his attempt to reconcile with Elise.

As he punched the doorbell, the thought of seeing Elise again had him twisted in knots. How many times had her tall, statuesque figure, pretty face and long brown hair streaked with honey-blond highlights come unbidden to his mind? How many nights had he dreamed about her and seen her brandy-colored eyes staring back at him? He couldn't count them. He'd handled things so badly with her. He'd pursued this job with the hopes of making things right, but would she give him the chance?

The doorbell sounded inside the house, shaking him from

his thoughts. Two females were playing havoc with his peace of mind. He wanted both of them in his life. Was that dream possible?

Seth took a deep breath as a shadowy figure appeared on the other side of the leaded glass in the front door. Tonight was supposed to be about a new job, but it also meant seeing Elise. He had to keep his head on straight.

The door swung open, and Ray motioned toward the interior of the house. "Seth, come in."

"Thanks for inviting me." Holding Olivia, Seth stepped into the entry hall, where a colorful area rug sat on the slate floor.

"And this young lady is your daughter?" Ray asked.

"Yes, she is." Seth set her down. "Say hello to Mr. Keller, Olivia."

Olivia clung to Seth's leg but didn't hesitate to speak. "Hello, Mr. Kewwa. I Olivia." She held up two fingers. "And I this many."

Ray, who had neatly trimmed brown hair without a trace of gray, hunkered down next to Olivia. "I'm very glad to meet you. I have two girls, but they're all grown up. Would you like to meet them?"

Olivia nodded, then glanced up at Seth, as if to seek his approval. "'Kay."

Ray turned his attention to Seth. "They're all back in the kitchen. Follow me."

Grabbing Olivia's hand, Seth took another deep breath and prepared to greet Elise. How would she react when she saw him? Since she'd left the cruise ship, she'd refused to talk with him, but she could hardly shun him while her family watched. Still, his heart raced as he followed Ray down the hall.

The sound of merriment floated from the kitchen. Seth immediately recognized Elise's throaty laugh. The sound made his heart trip. He swallowed a lump in his throat. Wishing he could untie the knots in his stomach, he gave himself a mental shake. He was putting too much stake in this meeting. He wasn't going to change Elise's opinion of him in one evening. Tonight was only one step in what was probably going to be a long journey.

His plan to explain things about his life now brought with it a flood of uncertainties. Had his selfish behavior in the past destroyed forever all traces of the love they had shared? Would she understand when he tried to tell her what had happened with Olivia? Would Elise even give him a chance to explain? He needed a lot of patience and time to show her he wasn't the man she used to know.

Delicious aromas floated through the air as Ray escorted Seth and Olivia into the kitchen. Seth remained silent as he stopped just inside the doorway and waited for Ray to open the conversation. Still holding Seth's hand, Olivia pulled his arm down. He glanced at her, then picked her up, balancing her in one arm as she wrapped her arms around his neck.

Ray waved a hand toward the three females occupying the kitchen. "Barbara, Juliane and Elise, I believe you all know Seth, but I'd like you to meet his daughter, Olivia."

Nodding, Seth didn't miss the way the color drained from Elise's face when she glanced at his little girl. The forced smile didn't mask the questions in Elise's eyes, but she didn't say a word, only nodded. He tried to relax as his gaze skimmed over Elise and settled on her mother.

He stepped forward and extended his hand to the petite middle-aged woman with short, light brown hair, liberally sprinkled with gray. "Hello, Barbara. It's good to see you again."

"We're glad you and Olivia could join us for dinner. I hope you like plain, old-fashioned cooking. We're having pot roast."

Seth smiled, feeling the tension in his shoulders loosen. "Sounds great! That's one of my favorites."

"One of my favorites, too." Ray chuckled as he patted his protruding middle. "As you can tell by the extra weight, my wife is an extraordinary cook."

Blushing, Barbara focused her attention on Olivia. "How about you, little girl? Do you like pot roast, as well?"

Clinging to Seth, Olivia laid her head on his shoulder. "She likes almost anything. You don't have to worry about her."

Straightening, Olivia looked at Barbara. "I a big girl and feed myself."

Olivia's pronouncement brought a smile to Barbara's face. "That's good to hear. I rounded up some small utensils for her to use earlier. Let me see if I can remember where I put them."

As Barbara turned and began searching in a nearby drawer, Juliane came around the kitchen's center island to shake his hand. With her chin-length light brown hair and caramel-colored eyes, she looked almost the same as the last time they'd met. The sisters' coloring was much the same, but Elise was tall and willowy while Juliane was at least a head shorter—petite like their mother. "Seth, good to see you again. Welcome to Kellerville. We're all so excited that you've taken the job."

"Thanks." Seth wondered whether *all* included Elise. He guessed from her expression that it didn't.

Although warmth radiated from the rich oak cabinets, granite countertops and homey oak furnishings in the room, there was no warmth in Elise's gaze. "Hello, Seth. How have you been?"

"I've been good—busy, but good." He couldn't help noticing that she was the only one who hadn't offered to shake his hand.

"I'm happy for you."

Seth tried to measure the sincerity of her words. Was she really glad, or was she being polite in front of her family? He doubted that her parents, or at least her dad, knew the whole story about the end of their relationship. If her parents knew, he probably wouldn't have gotten the job, much less this dinner invitation.

Olivia squirmed as Seth held her. "Down, please."

"Okay, here you go." Glad for Olivia's polite request, he gently deposited her on the hardwood floor, which matched the kitchen cabinets. When he glanced up, Elise was watching him. She immediately averted her eyes, as if she were embarrassed to have been caught staring at him. Wondering what she was thinking, he could hardly wait for the chance to talk with her alone. He didn't have a clue when that might happen. He had to get through this evening first.

On the other side of the kitchen, Elise looked down at her brown clogs. Seth had caught her staring. How was it possible that he had the little girl he'd refused to acknowledge eighteen months ago? She wanted to ask, but tonight's dinner wasn't the time for such a conversation, and she intended to see to it that they wouldn't meet again. Somehow she would get through this night. Then, hopefully, she wouldn't have to see Seth for any length of time. She'd just have to live without answers.

Elise shifted her gaze to the child. The sad, stricken face of the little girl's mother swam in Elise's mind as she looked at Olivia. She had her mother's big, dark brown eyes—the color of black coffee. Looking at the child made Elise relive that day in Key West—the day Seth had shown his true colors as he turned Olivia and her mother away. Elise tried to block the scene from her memory as a lump rose in her throat.

Turning from the drawer where she'd been rummaging, Barbara held up a small spoon and fork in triumph. "I found the things for Olivia. Just her size."

"Looks perfect." Ray held out a hand to Olivia. "Should we put them on the table by your plate?"

Barbara laughed as Olivia nodded and willingly followed Ray into the dining room. "Seth, I think Olivia has stolen my husband's heart. He's dying to be a grandparent like his brothers and sisters."

Juliane chuckled. "I think that's the pot calling the kettle black."

"Okay, you've got me there." Barbara glanced at Seth. "Seth, maybe you can let us borrow Olivia."

Seth smiled. "Does this mean you're offering to babysit? I'm going to miss having my mother around."

Barbara clasped her hands. "That's an excellent idea."

"I was kidding. I wouldn't want to impose."

"No imposition." Barbara looked at Ray, who had just returned to the kitchen with Olivia still clinging to his hand. "Ray and I would love to watch Olivia, wouldn't we?"

"I think that would be great!" Ray voice boomed through the kitchen.

Seth smiled as he glanced from Ray to Olivia. "Looks like you've got a new friend."

"Mr. Kewwa is nice." A little smile curved Olivia's mouth.

Being careful to keep a straight face, Elise smiled inwardly at Olivia's assessment. Maybe tonight wouldn't be so bad after all. Still, every time she looked at the child, she couldn't help remembering how badly Seth had behaved. What had changed? The question continued to haunt her.

Barbara retrieved a couple of dishes from the refrigerator and set them on the counter. "Ray and Juliane, please take these into the dining room and get everyone settled. Elise and I'll bring in the rest."

"Is there anything I can do to help?" Seth asked.

"No, thanks. You're a guest. We've got it covered, but I've

got something for Olivia." Barbara went into the pantry and returned a few seconds later with a bright red booster seat. She handed it to Seth. "You go into the dining room and get Olivia settled."

"Thanks." Seth took the booster seat, then glanced at Olivia. "Look what we've got. You want to help Daddy find a place at the table?"

"'Kay." Olivia scampered ahead.

Elise watched Seth follow his daughter, and her heart did a little flip-flop. She didn't want to have this reaction to him. She didn't want to feel anything for Seth—good or bad. She just wanted him somewhere else, but that was an impossible wish.

"Do I sense a little surprise from you about Olivia?" Barbara grabbed a big platter from the nearby cupboard and put the roast on it. "He told your father that you knew he had a daughter, but you seemed thrown at seeing her with him."

Surprised at her mother's perception, Elise stepped closer and put her back to the dining room so her voice wouldn't carry into the other room. She didn't want Seth to hear any of this conversation. "Do you intend to quiz me about Seth, or have me help you?"

"Both. You can put the potatoes and carrots in there." Barbara handed Elise a bowl. "So am I right?"

Elise didn't want to talk about it, but letting her mother know the truth was probably best. Still, there was no way Elise could possibly tell her mother the whole story. She didn't know the whole story herself. "Seth and I had a falling out just before I left my job on the cruise ship, and, yes, part of it had to do with Olivia. But at that time, he didn't have custody. Seeing her was surprising."

"I had no idea he had a child until he came here to interview. When did you find out?"

"This isn't the right time to talk about it."

"I agree, but for your father's sake, please make this a pleasant evening."

"I have no other intentions." Following her mother into the dining room, Elise prayed for God's peace to settle in her heavy heart.

When Elise reached the table, the only place left to sit was directly across from Seth. Still waiting for that peace she'd prayed for, she put the bowl on the table and took her seat. She didn't know which was worse—looking at Seth or at Olivia. They both filled her mind with troubling images from the past. Purging her thoughts of all disconcerting memories, she focused her attention on her father, who sat at the head of the table.

"It's so good to have my two girls here along with our guests. Let's thank God for this food and fellowship." Ray bowed his head.

As Elise bowed her head, she noticed that Olivia had bowed her head and folded her little hands. The sight touched Elise's heart. Was Olivia mimicking Ray, or had she learned about prayer from somewhere else? Elise doubted that Seth had encouraged Olivia to pray. When they'd been together, he'd had little use for God. Seth had never seen the point in believing in God or leaning on religion. She'd let him draw her away from the faith she'd known while growing up in Kellerville—a faith she had embraced again since her return—a faith that she hoped would see her through tonight and all future encounters with Seth Finley.

Chapter Two

Olivia giggled as Seth stood behind her chair, cutting the roast beef on her plate into little pieces and mashing her potatoes. He loved taking care of his daughter, but tonight what he really wanted was for Elise to notice that he was a changed man. He hoped his happy child would say something good about him. All he wanted was to prove himself to Elise, and maybe earn the chance to win back her love. She was the reason why he'd taken the job, why he'd moved to Kellerville. But given the way she'd worked to avoid him all evening, his chances looked pretty slim.

"Is that good?" Seth settled on the chair next to his daughter.

"Good, Daddy." Olivia picked up her fork and started to eat.

Seth cast a surreptitious glance in Elise's direction. She was helping herself to the potatoes and carrots and not paying the least bit of attention to him. Still, she looked tired and upset. Her manner reminded him that he needed to forget about his own worries. His selfish past was something he was trying to put behind him. If he was going to win her back, he'd need to remember to put Elise's feelings first. He was still working on that, and old habits seemed hard to overcome.

Juliane looked Seth's way. "Dad said you've been living in Pittsburgh, right?"

"Yes, I quit my job with the cruise line and moved back to Pittsburgh because my dad died suddenly from a heart attack. I knew my mom would need my help."

"Oh." Elise placed a hand over her heart. "I'm so sorry."

"Thanks. It was a real shock." Even after a year and a half, the trauma of his father's death still touched Seth. Sometimes, he thought, in his effort to be strong for his mother, he'd never let himself fully grieve.

"I knew you left the cruise line because of family problems. I didn't realize you'd lost your dad. I remember meeting him when your parents came on one of the cruises. He was terrific." Elise appeared truly sympathetic.

Seth let her reaction soak in. Maybe she still had a little soft spot in her heart for him. He could hope. "My dad's sudden death was very tough on my mom, so I wanted to be there for her."

Barbara passed the green beans to Elise. "How does your mom feel about your moving away now?"

"She's getting used to the idea."

Barbara glanced at Elise and Juliane, then back at Seth. "As a mom, I know how much I like having my girls close by. I didn't like Elise being so far away from home when she was working on the cruise ships."

"Neither did my mom." Seth chuckled. "Now she's more unhappy that Olivia won't be a few minutes away."

"I can understand that. If I had a granddaughter, I wouldn't want her far away, either." Barbara patted Seth on one arm.

After they finished passing the food, the conversation lagged for several minutes. As they started to eat, Seth didn't miss the looks Juliane gave Elise. What was that all about?

"Seth," Juliane said as she glanced at Elise, then back at him, "how did you happen to learn about the job here?"

Seth guessed the furtive glances that passed between the sisters had something to do with Juliane's question.

He wished Elise were the one who was curious about him coming here, not her sister. "Through a friend. A guy I worked with on one of the cruise ships moved to Cincinnati a few months ago. He contacted me to see whether I was interested in moving there."

Juliane raised her eyebrows. "But Kellerville isn't exactly Cincinnati."

"True, but he e-mailed me the link to the job board from the Cincinnati paper, and I saw the ad for the job here in Kellerville." Seth hoped Elise wasn't too angry that he'd taken the position. After he was hired, he'd promised himself that he wouldn't push for any contact with her right away. He wanted to win her back, but he knew he couldn't rush her. Anything that happened would have to be at Elise's pace. During the interview process, he made no effort to contact her, even when he'd been in town for interviews.

Juliane eyed him. "And you wanted to leave Pittsburgh?"

Seth wondered what Juliane was trying to accomplish with all of her questions. Was she trying to get him to admit that he'd come here because of Elise? "I did. I was looking for a new opportunity."

"So you thought Kellerville would be a good place for that opportunity?" Juliane continued her questioning like a scrappy little dog that had grabbed hold of a pant leg and wouldn't let go.

"Yeah." Guessing that Juliane was tackling the questions Elise wouldn't ask, Seth looked deliberately at her. "While we were working together, Elise used to talk about Kellerville and told me what a great little town it is."

With an expression of disbelief, Juliane turned to look at Elise. "You did?"

"Why are you so surprised?" Laying down her fork, Elise furrowed her eyebrows.

"Because you couldn't wait to leave."

"I know, but I came back, didn't I?"

"You did." Juliane smiled. "And I'm glad."

"Me, too."

Seth took in the exchange between the sisters, glad to have the attention on someone besides him. He guessed from their conversation that they'd buried old sibling rivalries. He remembered how Elise used to talk about Juliane always being the perfect one and how Elise could never hope to live up to her sister's image.

Seeing their newfound camaraderie, Seth wondered about the other changes he might find in Elise. He wanted to get to know her again. He hoped to have a new start with her just like the one she'd had with her sister.

Barbara took a sip of her water, then set the glass down. "I have to put in a plug for our wonderful little town, too. It's a great place to raise a child."

Seth glanced over at Olivia. "I thought that, too. Olivia was definitely a factor when I considered this job."

Ray slathered a roll with butter. "Well, the rec center committee, me included, is excited that you decided to take the position. Where are you staying now?"

"At that suites hotel on the edge of town."

"Nice place. Barbara's brother is the manager."

Seth smiled. "That's good to know. I'll be there until I can move into the house I've rented."

"When will that be?" Barbara asked.

"The moving van is supposed to arrive on Friday. I just hope there are no hang-ups. My stuff is on a truck that makes a delivery in Columbus before it comes here."

"Let us know if you need any help—like someone to watch Olivia." Barbara winked.

"Thanks. I might take you up on that."

"Please do." Barbara resumed eating.

The conversation lulled as everyone ate. In the quiet that ensued, Seth's mind buzzed with a myriad of thoughts about this move. He tried to put everything into perspective.

When Seth had found the job opening, he'd thought of it as a gift—a chance to get to know Elise again. He'd spent a lot of time in prayer. When he'd gotten the position, he'd seen it as an answer from God.

Now he was second-guessing himself. He knew that unless he could prove that he'd changed, she would hold his past against him.

Elise eyed him from across the table. "So if your mom isn't happy about your moving, why did you decide to leave Pittsburgh?"

Her question seemed to come out of the blue, and Seth didn't miss the accusation in it. Had she been sitting there sizing up the answers he'd given to her family's questions? Did she see his move as another selfish action? Maybe that soft spot he'd thought about earlier didn't exist after all.

"Most likely a move was in my future, whether I took this job or not."

"Why?" Elise sat forward as that little furrow between her eyebrows deepened.

"I was working for a hotel chain as a manager, and my boss indicated there was a transfer to Seattle in my future. So if I had to move, I wanted it to be on my terms, not someone else's. When my friend asked me about moving to Cincinnati, I saw the area as a good possibility. For my mom's sake, it isn't too far from Pittsburgh—about an hour by plane, or a little over four hours by car."

"Okay. Now I understand." Elise lowered her gaze and stabbed a piece of meat with her fork.

When she instantly ended their eye contact, Seth wondered whether she was embarrassed by the way she'd quizzed him about the move, or if she just wanted to avoid eye contact with him as much as possible.

He wanted her to like him again, but he could tell it would be a while before she'd be ready for a relationship with him again. First, he wanted a chance to apologize for being a jerk, then try to earn her respect. Thinking about the way he used to live always pained him. Even though God had forgiven him, he kept living with the guilt. Maybe gaining Elise's forgiveness would help him forgive himself.

Ray pushed back his chair and patted his stomach. "That was great food. You outdid yourself, dear."

"Thanks. I hope you left room for dessert." Barbara laid her napkin on the table. "I made a carrot cake."

"I've got plenty of room for carrot cake." Ray stood. "I'll help clear the table."

"I help, too." Olivia scrambled down from her chair.

Seth reached out and grabbed her arm. "Olivia, please ask Mrs. Keller whether she needs some help."

For a moment, Olivia looked crestfallen, and Seth's heart plummeted. She'd been so good. He didn't want anything to change that. But before he could say anything to soothe her concern, she brightened. "I help you?"

"I think that's a wonderful idea." Smiling, Barbara nodded and held out her hand to the little girl.

Thankful for Barbara's willingness to accept Olivia's request, Seth watched his child accompany Barbara to the kitchen. While they were gone, he helped the others clear the dining room table. Olivia's charm was working on everyone except Elise. He was still waiting to see her smile. His presence didn't appear to make her very happy. When she finally smiled, he would know he'd made some progress.

After they'd cleared the table, Barbara returned carrying a tray filled with plates, each containing a piece of cake. Olivia followed close behind. Gripping the edges of a white plastic plate, the little girl balanced the piece of cake, her steps slow and deliberate.

Olivia stopped beside Seth's chair. "For you, Daddy."

Seth took the plate. "Thank you, sweetheart. Do you want to get back in your seat?"

Olivia shook her head. "Help more."

Seth looked at Barbara. "Okay?"

"Sure." Barbara lowered the tray. "We'll serve together."

As Barbara carried the tray around the table, Olivia picked up the plates and gave one to each person. When they reached Elise, Olivia stood on her tiptoes and handed the plate to her. "'Lise, for you."

"Thank you, Olivia. You're such a good helper." Elise smiled as she took the plate.

Seth took in the smile. Though he wished it were for him, the smile warmed his heart. If she couldn't smile for him, at least she smiled for his daughter.

While they ate their cake, conversation floated around Seth. He made an occasional comment, but he mostly listened, taking in the joy. He was glad Elise had found happiness back in her hometown. He wondered whether he could ever be a part of it.

Ray finished a bite of cake, then glanced at Seth. "I'll have to introduce you to our future son-in-law, Lukas. He would've been here tonight, but he had to attend some kind of management meeting at the medical devices plant he runs."

Seth's heart nearly stopped as a bite of cake went down wrong. Was Elise engaged? He'd never considered the possibility that she might have found a new love since returning home. Having to watch her with someone else would be a cruel turn of events.

"I'm sure Lukas will try to recruit you for the church softball team," Juliane said, tucking a strand of hair behind her ear.

As Seth looked at Juliane, he noticed the sparkling diamond ring on her left hand. Lukas must be Juliane's fiancé. A cautious relief settled around his heart. Seth checked Elise's left hand. No ring, but that didn't mean she wasn't dating someone. He was every kind of fool for thinking he could waltz into town and find his way into her heart again with no obstacles.

"I'm sure Seth isn't interested in being on the church softball team." Elise didn't even look at him as she made the statement.

"But I would. Sounds like fun." Seth waited for Elise's reaction, but none came.

"I've got a great idea." Ray snapped his fingers. "There's a men's prayer breakfast before church tomorrow. Would you like to go with me? Since you're new in town, the gathering would be a good opportunity to meet Lukas and a bunch of the other guys."

"Dad, you're being a little pushy, aren't you?" Elise's gaze darted between Seth and her father.

"Really, Elise, your dad's right. I'd like to meet some folks from the community." Seth didn't miss the surprise in Elise's eyes. Was she remembering the old Seth—the one who had no use for God or religion?

"Great. I can pick you up at the hotel," Ray said.

Seth glanced at Olivia. "Like I said before, I'd like to join you, but I can't take Olivia to the men's prayer breakfast."

Barbara looked expectantly at Seth. "Oh…this could be my first chance to babysit. I can watch Olivia while you go to the breakfast."

Seth hesitated again. Even though Olivia seemed comfortable with Barbara, he wasn't sure how Olivia would act for a lengthy time with someone she didn't know very well. Her sitters in Pittsburgh had always been his mother or his aunt Susan. But he had to face the fact that he'd have to rely on a lot of new people here to help him with his child. Having Barbara watch Olivia was probably a good start.

"What do you say, Olivia? Would you like to visit with Mrs. Keller in the morning while Daddy goes to a meeting?"

Olivia shrugged her little shoulders. "'Kay."

Seth recognized her uncertainty and tried to reassure her. "You'll have a good time."

Barbara smiled at Olivia. "Do you like pancakes?"

Olivia nodded.

"Good. You and I can make pancakes for breakfast. Would you like that?"

Olivia nodded again.

Barbara turned her attention to Seth. "You can bring her out here in the morning before you go to the breakfast."

"The breakfast starts at eight o'clock at my cousin's café. Do you remember the one on Main Street where we had lunch with Nathan?" Ray asked.

"I do."

"Then we'll see you there. I know you'll enjoy meeting the other men."

Barbara motioned toward the little girl. "When you come in the morning, you can leave Olivia's car seat with me, and I'll bring her when I come to church. They have an excellent class for two- and three-year-olds, if you think she'll go."

"We can wait and see on that one," Seth replied.

Olivia clamored into Seth's lap and laid her little head on his chest. He glanced down. Seth's heart warmed as his daughter snuggled close. He hoped this move would prove to be a good choice for his little girl.

"I think someone's sleepy." Barbara patted the top of Olivia's head.

"I think you're right. If I'm going to get up early for the prayer breakfast, I should head back to the hotel." Seth smiled down at Olivia, then glanced at Barbara as he stood. "Thanks so much for the wonderful meal. I enjoyed the evening."

Everyone joined Seth near the front door as he helped Olivia get into her little jacket.

"See you in the morning." Ray waved as he stood on the front porch with his arm around Barbara's waist.

Seth waved in return, then buckled Olivia into her car seat. As he backed his car out of the driveway, the Kellers waved again, even Elise. She appeared to be smiling. Had he made a little progress, or was she glad he was leaving?

He had to quit second-guessing himself. He hoped tomorrow's appearance at church would help Elise see him as a changed man. He should remember to pray for patience where she was concerned.

Talk about an emotional roller-coaster ride—tonight had been one!

"What do you know about Seth's little girl?" Barbara started clearing the dessert plates from the table as soon as they came inside.

Elise had expected her mother to ask these questions sooner or later, but she'd hoped they would come later—maybe after she knew more herself. "You should've asked Seth."

Barbara frowned. "I couldn't ask him."

"Why not? He has the answers."

"I couldn't put him on the spot or embarrass him. He was our guest."

Knowing more questions would follow, Elise decided to put the truth out there for the whole family to hear. "The last I knew, he wasn't willing to marry Olivia's mother or even acknowledge that the child was his. I don't know what happened since then or why he has Olivia now."

"Oh." Averting her eyes, Barbara lowered her head.

Elise surmised that her mother's loss for words meant she was both shocked and curious at the same time. An uncomfortable silence filled the kitchen.

Ray cleared his throat. "I'll make sure to ask Seth at the prayer breakfast."

Elise turned to her father. "Dad, please don't ask any embarrassing questions."

"Baby girl, don't you know I'm only kidding?" Ray chuckled.

Sighing, Elise tried not to let her dad's teasing annoy her. "This isn't a joking matter."

Ray nodded. "I know, but I had to break the morbid silence somehow. Besides, I've learned that stating the truth is always the best solution. Letting people know about my alcohol problem has been very freeing."

"That's true, but you did that in your own time. Seth will do the same when it comes to Olivia." Elise sighed heavily. "This whole business with Seth has been upsetting."

Ray placed some plates in the dishwasher. "I knew you might not be happy that he was moving here, but I think it'll do you good to deal with the past so you can finally put it behind you."

"You discussed this with Juliane, didn't you? I'm not happy that you all have been talking about me behind my back." Elise shot a pointed glance at her dad and her sister, then grabbed a dishrag and started wiping the counters. She wished she could wipe away all this mess with Seth, too.

"Honey." Her dad put a hand on her shoulder. "If I'd thought it was a bad thing, I never would've agreed with the committee to hire Seth. In fact, the reason I discussed it with your sister was to get her advice."

Elise stopped scrubbing and glared at Juliane. "And you told him to go ahead?"

"I explained that to you. I thought you needed to get over the past." Juliane put the last glass in the dishwasher.

"I have, and I've moved on with my life." Elise resumed washing the counter.

Juliane put soap in the dispenser, then turned to Elise. "I mean, you need to *face* the past, not bury it."

Pressing her lips together, Elise shook her head. "One thing's for certain. Nothing stays buried with you around."

Juliane frowned. "Elise, please don't be angry with me."

Trying to gain control over her emotions, Elise wrung out the dishrag. "I'm not angry, just... I don't even know how to describe my feelings."

"I love you, little sis." Juliane gave Elise a hug.

Elise smiled and hugged her back. "Me, too."

Ray chuckled. "I'm glad you girls have grown up. This would not be the way you would've handled this situation when you were in high school."

"So true. We might have had a little hair pulling." Barbara laughed out loud. "But, no matter the circumstances, that little Olivia is the cutest thing, and she looks so much like Seth. He seems to be trying to do the right thing now. Give him a chance."

"Okay. You've all made your points, but there's a big knot of pain right here." Elise tapped a fist over her heart. "Seeing Seth again made it worse."

Ray put an arm around Elise's shoulders. "I just want you to be happy, baby girl."

Leaning into her father, Elise closed her eyes for a moment, then glanced up at him. "I know, Dad. But please don't try to fix the situation. I can work through this on my own."

"I didn't mean to bring you any trouble." Her dad held her close. "I certainly didn't want to hurt you."

"I understand that, but I want *you* to understand my mind-set." Elise took a deep breath and let it out slowly. "Seth is a tireless worker, a real charmer and a people person, so I can see why you hired him. I'm sure he's a perfect choice for this job. But that doesn't mean I have to be involved. So it would be a lot easier in the future if you left me off the guest list for any function where he'll be in attendance, okay?"

Ray shook his head. "I'll do my best, but this is a small town. You can't expect to avoid him."

Elise laughed halfheartedly. "I'm aware of that, but I'd rather keep my distance, if possible."

"Is Olivia the reason you ended your relationship with Seth?" Concern knit Barbara's brow.

"Partly, but I really don't want to discuss it. I don't want my thoughts about Seth to color yours." Elise searched their faces. "He deserves a fresh start here, so let's drop the subject, okay?"

Juliane folded a dish towel and hung it on the nearby rack. "Does this mean you're not going to be on the softball team if Seth joins?"

Elise laughed, feeling her tension fade. She hadn't realized how wired she'd been while Seth was there until now. "Your only concern is the church softball team?"

"Well, you *are* the best pitcher we have. You were our ace last year."

"Surely you won't miss me if I don't play this year."

"Lukas is counting on you."

"Well, maybe if he's super, super nice to me." Elise's only thought was finding a way to keep Lukas from asking Seth to join the team. She had little hope of that. She had to face facts. As long as Seth lived in Kellerville, she would have to get used to being around him. She'd better start praying now for strength to deal with him.

Chapter Three

After saying good-night to her folks, Elise rushed to Juliane's car. Elise had little doubt that her sister would ply her with all kinds of questions on the way home. Despite her plea not to talk about Seth, Elise knew Juliane wouldn't quit asking until she got some answers.

Juliane hurried to keep up with Elise. "I was curious about you and Seth before, but after this evening, you have to explain everything."

"I'm surprised you waited this long to ask. I thought you'd corner me in the pantry and twist my arm."

"Not possible." Juliane chuckled. "You're bigger than I am. So what gives?"

"I'm not sure I can explain anything. I'm just as confused as you are about Olivia."

As Juliane opened the driver's-side door, she looked over the top of the car at Elise. "What's confusing about Olivia?"

"Everything. I don't know why he has the child he rejected. My explanation isn't going to help you understand it. So what's the point?"

Juliane gave her a stern look as she got into the car. "While

I drive home, you're *going* to tell me what happened between you and Seth. I won't take no for an answer. No excuses."

Elise plopped onto the bucket seat and yanked the door closed. While Juliane drove down the lane to the main road, Elise tried to gather her thoughts. Where did she start? Maybe with the sordid truth. "Well, here it is in a nutshell. Seth Finley is a womanizer. He had a woman in every port. And the fact that he has a child tells you he wasn't just talking with them."

"If he was so terrible, why were you dating him?"

"Because he had me fooled—probably like all the other women in his life. Like Olivia's mother."

"You knew Olivia's mother?"

"I didn't know her personally. I saw her once—the day she showed up with Olivia."

"And you were there?"

Nodding, Elise sighed heavily.

"How did that happen?"

Elise stared straight ahead into the darkness and let the painful memory float through her mind.

She glanced at Juliane. "Okay. Here's what I know. We were docked in Key West and had some free time, so we had lunch on the patio of one of our favorite restaurants."

"So what happened?"

"If you'd quit interrupting, I'd tell you."

"Okay, I'll be quiet."

"Anyway, while we were talking, this pretty woman with long black hair and the darkest brown eyes I've ever seen walked up to us. She was pushing a stroller containing a child who looked to be about a year old." Elise swallowed a lump in her throat.

"Was this Olivia's mother?" Juliane asked.

Elise nodded. "Seth tried to ignore her at first, but she wouldn't let him. She insisted he come out and talk to her."

"So did he?"

"Yeah, because she wasn't going away until he did. Besides, she was attracting the attention of nearby diners. He was clearly upset when he got up and went to meet her. He guided her halfway down the block. Although I couldn't hear exactly what they were saying, I could tell by their expressions and raised voices that they were arguing."

"What happened then?"

"Seth reached into his pocket and pulled out some money and gave it to her, then turned and walked away. When she followed him and grabbed his arm, he shook her off and told her to get lost."

"So what did you do?"

"I was dying inside while I watched them. I felt so sorry for that woman and wondered whether he would treat me that way someday. I couldn't believe how he was acting." Elise pressed a hand to her chest.

"Did you ask him what was going on?"

"Of course. He told me he didn't want to discuss it—that it wasn't any of my business." Telling this story brought back the pain. Even though Olivia had obviously been conceived before Elise and Seth had made the move from flirtation to relationship, Elise had still felt betrayed. Seth had clearly known about the baby, and yet he had never even mentioned the child to her before. The man she'd thought of as generous and caring had quite literally turned his back on his daughter, and on the woman who had been his lover, and instead of offering any explanation for his behavior to Elise, he'd pushed her away.

"What did you do then?"

"I got up and left."

"Did he come after you?"

"He did, and he tried to convince me the woman wasn't anyone I needed to concern myself about, that the baby wasn't his, anyway."

"Did you believe him?"

"I loved him, Juliane. I'd given him my heart and soul. And more." Pausing, Elise swallowed hard as she twisted her hands in her lap. "Please don't think I'm terrible. We were sleeping together. I wanted to believe our relationship was important to him, but how could I when he refused to tell me what was going on, why he'd behaved so horribly? The more I asked, the angrier he got, until finally, he stormed out."

As Juliane stopped the car at a traffic light, she reached across the console and patted Elise's arm. "We've all done things in our lives we wish we hadn't."

"Do you understand now why I didn't want to see him again? The relationship I thought we had was proven false. He wasn't the man I thought he was, and it still hurts to look at him and remember that."

"Do you still love him?"

Elise didn't want to answer. Her mind buzzed with conflicting thoughts. No. No. No. Surely she didn't still love him. She couldn't love a man who treated women the way he'd treated her and Olivia's mother. "How could I?"

"You obviously have some kind of feelings for him."

"Conflicting ones. I don't want him to mess up my life again."

"He can't if you don't let him."

"Well, I plan to steer clear of him as much as possible."

Juliane pulled her car into the garage of the little century-old house that she and Elise shared near the heart of town. "Thanks for telling me. Now I understand some of what you're feeling."

"Please don't mention this to Mom and Dad." Elise followed Juliane into the house.

Juliane flipped on the light in the kitchen. "Okay, but don't you wonder why he has Olivia?"

"Yeah, but I'm not going there. That's his business, not mine or yours."

"But don't you wish you knew?"

Elise eyed her sister. "Juliane, you'd better let it go, or I won't help you address your wedding invitations."

"Okay, you win."

"Nothing about this feels like winning." Elise hung her jacket on the hook by the kitchen door. As she walked into the living room, the doorbell rang.

"That's Lukas. He said he'd stop by after his meeting." Juliane rushed past Elise.

Elise reached out and grabbed Juliane's arm. "Please don't say anything about Seth to Lukas, either."

"My lips are sealed." Juliane pretended to turn a key on her lips like they'd done when they were kids.

"Thanks, sis." Elise headed for the stairs. "I've got some studying to do, so I'll leave you lovebirds alone."

As Juliane answered the door, Elise raced up the stairs. She didn't want to take the chance that Lukas would ask about the evening, because the conversation might involve Seth.

Standing in the choir room before the beginning of the worship service the following morning, Elise dreaded the thought of seeing Seth again. He'd be sitting out there in the pews somewhere. Could she avoid looking at him while she stood at the front of the sanctuary with the praise team during the song service?

She wasn't sure why he was doing the church routine. He certainly hadn't been a churchgoer when they'd worked together. Maybe his church attendance now was more about impressing her dad than anything else.

While those thoughts buzzed in Elise's mind, Juliane approached. "Have you seen Lukas? I can't find him anywhere.

He's scheduled to sing with the praise team this morning. We talked about it last night."

Elise glanced around the room. "Did he go to the prayer breakfast this morning?"

Juliane shrugged. "He'd planned to go, but even if he did, they always finish in plenty of time for the men to get to church."

"I haven't seen Dad, either." *Or Seth.* Elise didn't want to voice that thought aloud.

Elise's mother rushed into the room. "Something terrible has happened."

"What?" Elise stared at her mother's stricken face.

Pressing her fingers to her lips, Barbara didn't speak for a moment in what appeared to be an attempt to control her emotions. "Your dad called—"

"Did something happen to Dad?" Elise took hold of her mother's arm.

Barbara shook her head. "It's Seth."

Elise's heart plummeted, and her pulse began to pound. "What about Seth?"

"He was in a terrible car accident."

"Is he…is he okay?" Elise could hardly breath.

"I don't know." Barbara shook her head again. "Your dad said they rushed him to the hospital. He's in emergency surgery right now. That's all I know."

"Where did it happen?" Elise asked.

"About a mile from our house. You know the spot where there's a small rise in the road?" Barbara touched a hand to her forehead as if trying to make sense of everything.

Elise nodded. "I know the place. Was Olivia with him?"

Shaking her head, Barbara clasped her hands. "Praise God, Seth had already dropped her off with me. He was on his way back into town when it happened."

As Elise took in the information, her heart ached. She'd

been upset that Seth was back in her life, but she'd never wanted anything like this to happen to him. "Do you know how it happened?"

"Your dad wasn't sure, but from what they could tell, Seth's car skidded off the road, probably because of the rain. The car crashed into a tree, and he was trapped inside. They had to use the Jaws of Life to get him out. It took over an hour." Barbara turned to Juliane. "Lukas is waiting for news at the hospital."

"Where's Olivia?" Elise asked.

Barbara turned back to Elise. "I dropped Olivia off in the class for her age as soon as I got here. Your father called right after that, so she knows nothing about her dad."

"That poor little girl…in a strange place with people she barely knows." Elise wrinkled her brow as she realized the child wouldn't understand what was happening. "How will we explain everything to her?"

Barbara took a deep breath. "We need to leave that to her grandmother."

"But she isn't here, is she?" Elise glanced toward the door.

"No, but while Seth was trapped in the car, he was still coherent enough to give your dad his mom's phone number." Barbara paused to catch her breath. "Your dad called her, and she was able to book a flight that gets into Cincinnati around one o'clock. Your dad's going to the airport to pick her up."

Mind whirling, Elise digested all that her mother was saying. Now she would have to face Seth's mother, as well as Seth. Elise remembered her from the times Seth's parents had taken a cruise on the ship where Seth and she had been working. "How did Dad know about the accident?"

"After Seth didn't show up for the prayer breakfast, your dad called me to find out whether he'd dropped off Olivia as he'd planned. When I told him Seth had already dropped her off, he and Lukas suspected something must be wrong."

"How did they know where to look for him?" Elise asked.

"They figured maybe Seth had car trouble. A flat tire or something like that, but not a horrific accident." Barbara released a harsh breath. "They drove along the route that Seth would've taken from our house to the café. That's when they came upon the accident."

"Thank the Lord they were smart enough to go looking. Otherwise, no telling how long it would have been before someone came along." Elise shoved away the thought of what might have happened if her dad hadn't gone to search for Seth.

"If they hadn't found him, I may have been the first person to come upon the accident on my way to church." Barbara laid a hand on her chest. "I don't know whether I could've handled that. And worse yet, Olivia would've been with me."

"We don't have to think about that." Elise hugged her mom. "Should we go to the hospital?"

"I'm going to call Lukas and see whether he knows anything." Juliane fished her cell phone out of her purse.

Barbara touched Juliane's arm. "There's no point in calling Lukas. Your dad told me they expected Seth to be in surgery for several hours."

Elise glanced from Juliane to her mother. "Then what can we do?"

At that moment, the music minister, Tom Porter, came over to the group. "Did I hear you say something about someone in the hospital?"

After Barbara gave a condensed version of Seth's situation, Tom asked for other prayer requests. Then he had the group join hands as he led them in prayer.

Elise managed to get through the song service, but she

couldn't concentrate on the sermon. Her mind kept imagining Seth clinging to life as he lay in the hospital. She'd spent too many days wishing never to set eyes on Seth again. Now she could hardly wait until the church service ended so she could go to the hospital and see him.

The heels of Elise's shoes clicked on the tile floor and echoed through the lobby of the hospital. Without waiting for Juliane, she turned down the hallway leading to the surgery wing.

"Hey, there's no sense in being in such a hurry. Lukas said Seth still isn't out of surgery." Juliane raced to keep up with Elise.

"I know, but nerves are making me hyper." Elise turned the corner. "There's Lukas."

Lukas stood as soon as he saw them. He met them halfway as they approached the surgery waiting room. "No word yet."

Elise hugged Lukas, then stepped back. "Was it bad?"

Lukas nodded as he pulled Juliane close and gave her a kiss on the cheek. Taking her hand, he led them toward the chairs lining the wall. His coal-black hair contrasted with Juliane's light brown hair. "I don't know how he survived that crash. His car was practically wrapped around the tree. The whole passenger side was crushed in, and he was trapped in this little space on the driver's side."

Elise's stomach churned as she listened. Sitting next to Juliane, Elise forced herself to ask the dreaded question that kept resurfacing in her mind. "Is he going to be all right?"

"I wish I could say for certain." Lukas squeezed Juliane's hand.

With a hint of envy, Elise watched Juliane and Lukas. Elise wished she had someone to hold her hand and comfort her. Still, Elise was happy that her sister had found someone to love who treated her with kindness and respect. She had thought she'd found someone like that in Seth, but she'd been wrong. After the way he'd abandoned his child, she'd found herself second-guessing everything, wondering if anything he'd promised her, even his love, was real and lasting.

Answers hadn't come, no matter how many nights she lay awake wondering. Seth, who had left the ship shortly after their fight for a family emergency that she now knew was about his father, hadn't been there to offer any explanations or assurances, leaving her prey to the worst of her doubts and insecurities. By the time she left the cruise ship herself, she'd been convinced that Seth had never really loved her and had tried to close her heart off to him in turn. As she sat in the waiting room, desperate for news, she started to wonder if her feelings hadn't changed as much as she'd thought.

Elise leaned forward to look at Lukas, who sat on the other side of Juliane. "Mom said they expected Seth to be in surgery for several hours. How long has it been?"

Lukas glanced at his watch. "A couple of hours at least."

A helpless feeling washed over Elise. "Is that good or bad?"

"You're asking me stuff I can't begin to answer."

Elise gave Lukas a halfhearted smile. "I'm sorry. I wish someone could tell us what's going on."

"We'll probably have to wait until they're done with the surgery to know how he is." Juliane patted Elise's arm.

Elise released a heavy sigh. "I know, but I hate this waiting."

"You want to go to the cafeteria and get something to eat?" Lukas asked.

Elise shook her head. "If we leave, we might miss the doctor."

Lukas stood. "Do you want me to go and bring something back for you?"

"Thanks. That would be great, sweetheart." Juliane smiled up at him.

After Lukas took their orders and left, Elise paced back and forth. She stopped and glanced out the window at the rain-soaked landscape. Her mom had said something about Seth's car skidding on the rain-slick road. Elise shuddered at the thought.

Even the colorful parade of daffodils and crocuses that filled the flowerbeds near the hospital entrance couldn't brighten Elise's thoughts. The gray April day captured her mood.

While Elise paced in front of the window, Juliane walked over and gently took hold of her arm to pull her to a stop. "You know pacing and worrying aren't going to change anything."

Elise stopped and looked at her sister. "I have to walk off my nerves."

"For someone who said she never wanted to see Seth again, you seem awfully worried about him."

"I'm not sure what I'm feeling." Elise sank onto a nearby chair. "I loved him, so I don't want anything awful to happen to him, especially since he has that sweet little girl. She obviously adores him."

"And what about you?"

Elise didn't want to examine her feelings or answer her sister's question. Did love for Seth still occupy her heart? She pushed that thought away. "Didn't we have this conversation once before?"

"Yeah, but I still have questions."

"And I don't have any answers."

"Humor me."

Elise looked down the hallway. Where was Lukas? His return would rescue her from Juliane's curiosity. "There's not much humor in this story."

"Just answer this. Did you ever learn the truth about Olivia's mother?"

"Not the entire story." Elise stared out the window again. "I told you before that he said that the woman just wanted money, that Olivia wasn't his, even though I could clearly see that she looked just like him, even then. But his behavior killed a little part of my heart and my feelings for him."

"So you dumped him right then?"

"Yes. I still had thirty days left on my contract with the cruise line, or I would have left that day. It about killed me to think about being on the same ship with Seth for another month. As the cruise director, his presence would have been hard to avoid. But he left just a few days later when he got word about his father. All the same, I barely got through the month."

"That's why you looked so awful when you returned home."

"Oh, thanks."

"You know what I mean. You were so thin."

"Well, I'm back to my normal weight now, and life here is good. I don't want Seth Finley's presence in town to change that. But what kind of person would I be if I ignored Seth while he was in dire straits? My actions wouldn't be any better than his, when he ignored Olivia's mother. Even if it's hard for me, I've got to do what I know to be the right thing."

Juliane leaned over and put an arm around Elise's shoulders. "Remember, I'm here for you anytime you need someone to talk to."

"I know. That's been one of the great things about coming back home."

"I agree. You managed to help me keep my head when I was dealing with Lukas. Maybe I can do the same for you while you're working through this." Juliane glanced down the hallway. "Here comes Lukas with the food."

"Good. My stomach's beginning to rumble." But even as she made the statement, Elise wondered whether she would be able to eat.

After Lukas passed out the food, they ate in silence, and Elise replayed her conversation with Juliane. Elise was glad they'd talked, but she wasn't sure even Juliane's counsel would get her through her confusion over Seth. And when was someone going to tell them what was happening with him?

Chapter Four

Time dragged. Elise paced. Her mind buzzed. When she thought she couldn't stand another minute of the waiting, she saw her father and Seth's mother, Maggie Finley, hurrying down the hallway. She looked the same as the last time Elise had seen her about two years ago.

Maggie's trim figure and dark brown hair belied her age, but her ashen and haggard expression spelled out her worry. Elise wondered what she could possibly say to Seth's mother. Did she know how their relationship had ended? No matter. This wasn't the time to think about herself.

Ray hugged his daughters, then glanced around the waiting area. "Still no word?"

Lukas stepped forward. "We haven't heard a thing and have to assume Seth is still in surgery."

Maggie sank onto a nearby chair. "Can't we ask someone?"

"Let me check." Ray strode back down the hallway.

Maggie turned her attention to Elise. "Hello, Elise."

"Hi, Mrs. Finley." Taking a seat in a nearby chair, Elise tried to pull up a smile. "I can't believe this has happened to Seth. We've been praying for him."

"Thank you. I appreciate it." Maggie shook her head. "I can't believe this has happened, either."

Before Elise could respond, Ray returned with Barbara, who carried Olivia. Nathan, Pastor Tom and Pastor Rob, the senior minister, accompanied them.

"Olivia." Maggie jumped up and raced to greet her granddaughter. She reached out for the child and hugged her as the little girl went eagerly into Maggie's arms. "Grandma's so glad to see you."

"Gramma." Olivia put her arms around Maggie's neck.

The scene touched Elise's heart. She tried to put herself in Maggie's place. She had to be anxious about her son's condition but thankful that her grandchild hadn't been in harm's way. Elise recalled how Seth mentioned that his mother wasn't thrilled with his move. How would she view this latest development? What would happen now?

While Elise pondered the future, her dad took charge and introduced Maggie to everyone. After he made the last introduction, Pastor Rob led the group in a prayer for Seth. When the prayer was over, the group fell silent except for Olivia. She began crying for Seth.

Maggie took a seat again and tried to comfort the child. "Olivia, honey, you can't see your daddy right now because the doctors are fixing his boo-boos."

"He has boo-boo?"

Nodding, Maggie held Olivia close. "We have to wait till he's better to see him."

The scene tore Elise up inside. Remembering Seth's interaction with his daughter during dinner the previous evening, Elise prayed Seth would be all right for the sake of his little girl. She needed her daddy. Even as Elise thought about Seth's recovery, she couldn't help wondering about Olivia's mother. What had happened to her?

While Elise tried to make sense of why Seth now had the

child he'd rejected, she remained quiet as everyone talked around her. She had a difficult time focusing on any of the conversations. Her thoughts centered on Seth, in spite of herself.

Barbara's brow knit in a frown as she talked to Maggie. "Where are you planning to stay?"

"I suppose in the hotel where Seth was staying." Maggie shrugged.

Barbara laid a hand on one of Maggie's arms. "We can't have you staying out there. Now that Elise and Juliane are gone from home, Ray and I are rattling around in our big old house. We have plenty of room, and it'll be so much better for you to stay with us, especially since you have Olivia with you."

"Oh, we couldn't impose on you. You barely know us."

"No problem. We'll get to know you." Barbara reached for her purse and pulled out a pen and paper. "I'll give you our phone number."

"But—"

"I won't take no for an answer."

"If you insist."

Ray walked over. "I can take you to the hotel so you can get Olivia's and Seth's things."

"You folks are being too kind." Maggie smiled even while unshed tears sparkled in her eyes.

Elise took in the scene with a pinprick of dread. She was proud of her parents' generosity but worried that her mother's hospitality would mean more association with Seth. As she tried to squash the self-absorbed thought, she caught movement out of the corner of her eye. Looking in that direction, she spied Bill Daubenmire, an orthopedic surgeon, who was a member of their church.

Still dressed in his scrubs, the tall, dark-haired doctor approached them. Her heart racing, she gripped the arms of her chair in order to keep from rocketing out of it and demanding answers from him. She tried to read his expression, but it told her nothing.

"Dr. Daubenmire." Ray motioned toward Maggie. "This is Seth Finley's mother, Maggie."

Still holding Olivia, Maggie shook the doctor's hand. "Doctor, what can you tell me about Seth?"

The doctor's expression brightened, and a slight smile curved his mouth. "Mrs. Finley, Seth's in recovery, and his prognosis is guardedly optimistic."

Maggie patted Olivia's back. "When can I see him?"

"Soon. I'll have one of the nurses let you know when he's out of recovery." Dr. Daubenmire motioned down the hallway. "He'll be in ICU for at least forty-eight hours, then, hopefully, we can move him to a regular room."

"Do you know how long he'll be in the hospital?" Maggie asked.

"Since he's a relatively young man, I expect him to recover fairly fast, but I don't want to make any predictions at this point." Dr. Daubenmire looked over the group, then back at Maggie. "If you'd like, I can tell you exactly what we did today during surgery."

Maggie nodded. "Please. I would appreciate that."

"Okay." Dr. Daubenmire nodded. "We can talk while we head toward the ICU."

"I'll take Olivia for you." Barbara held out her arms for the little girl.

"Thank you." Maggie hugged Olivia. "Grandma's going to leave you with Miss Barbara for a few minutes, okay?"

"'Kay." Olivia bobbed her little head.

"I'll be back very soon." Maggie placed Olivia in Barbara's open arms, then waved as she left with Dr. Daubenmire.

Elise marveled at the way her mother had been able to befriend Olivia in such a short time. Elise could see her mother growing attached to the child already. That attachment didn't have to involve Elise, but she feared it would.

Elise looked down and saw the white-knuckled grip she still had on the arm of the chair. Releasing a slow breath, she loosened her hold and eased back in the chair. Seth was going to be okay.

While the conflicting emotions battled in Elise's heart and mind, she tried to put the whole thing into perspective. Only a day ago she'd raged against the idea of seeing Seth. She'd wanted nothing to do with him. Now she wanted nothing more than to see him. How was that possible?

Machines, tubes and wires surrounded Seth as he lay on the hospital bed, thankful to be alive. He could move his fingers and his toes. He wasn't sure about the rest of his body parts, but the fingers and toes gave him hope for the rest.

The nurses told him he was doing fine, but the pain medication was making him a little groggy. He had a vague memory of the doctor telling him about the surgery to mend his broken leg and other injuries. Events surrounding the accident flitted in and out of his mind. He couldn't seem to focus on any of them. He mostly remembered Ray Keller encouraging him and praying while the rescue team worked to extract him from the wreckage. He closed his eyes and thanked God for sparing his life for Olivia's sake. He wanted to live for that little girl.

"Seth."

At the sound of the soft female voice, Seth opened his eyes. His mother stood beside his bed. "Hi, Mom."

Tears shimmering in her eyes, she stared at him. "How are you?"

"Alive."

"Thank the Lord for that." She reached for his hand and

squeezed it. "I can't believe this happened to you. I caught a plane as soon as I got the call."

"Where's Olivia?"

"She's out in the waiting area with the Kellers."

"Why didn't you bring her to see me?"

Maggie waved a hand toward the bed. "I didn't want her to see you like this."

"Do I look that bad?"

"What do you think?"

"I don't have any idea how I look." Seth slowly shook his head.

"Well, you look like you've been in a terrible accident. Besides, I don't think Olivia would understand all the tubes and wires." Maggie patted his arm. "I wouldn't want to scare her."

Closing his eyes, Seth nodded his head. "I suppose you're right."

"I'm hoping she can see you when you are transferred to a regular room."

Seth opened his eyes. "Did the doctor say when that would be?"

"He hoped forty-eight hours. Didn't he tell you?"

"Maybe. I've been very groggy. It hurts to think."

"Don't think." Maggie patted his arm again. "Would you like to see Elise?"

"She's here?"

Maggie nodded. "She's out in the waiting room with her family."

Seth let that information drift through his fuzzy brain. Despite Elise's less than enthusiastic reception at her parents' house, she was here. Could that possibly mean she cared for him, at least a little? "Does she want to see me?"

"She's here, isn't she? If she didn't want to see you, I doubt she'd be here."

Seth tried to smile. "I don't want to scare her."

"I think she's old enough to handle seeing your injuries." Maggie returned his smile. "It's good to see you still have your sense of humor."

"Don't make her come to see me if she doesn't want to."

"I don't think you have to worry about that."

"Are you sure?" Seth wanted to believe his mother, but he kept remembering Elise's reaction at dinner the previous evening.

"You know I wasn't for this move, but after seeing the caring way people have reacted to your accident, I realize I was wrong." Maggie gave Seth's hand another squeeze. "The doctor said we had to limit our visitation time, so I'll go get Elise."

Seth watched his mother leave, then closed his eyes.

When he blinked his eyes open a little while later, Seth wondered whether he was dreaming or whether the woman staring out the window as she sat on the nearby chair was just a painkiller-induced mirage.

He squeezed his eyes shut, then opened them. She was still there. "Elise?"

She turned and looked at him. "Seth, you're awake."

"Yeah." He tried to smile, but even that simple motion brought discomfort. "How long have you been here?"

She stood but didn't come closer to the bed. Her shoulders rigid, she appeared ill at ease. "A few minutes. Your mom said I could see you."

"I must've drifted off. It's hard to keep my eyes open." He wondered how bad he looked. Was that why she appeared so uncomfortable, or did being with him make her uncomfortable?

"I didn't want to disturb you." Elise took a step closer to the bed.

Seth closed his eyes for a moment and pushed away his

earlier negative thoughts. He let Elise's presence fill him with hope. God did answer prayers, but Seth knew he still needed to practice caution. Elise had always been a compassionate person. That was part of what had drawn him to her. And it was part of why he'd lost her. She couldn't tolerate the way he'd treated Olivia's mother. True, he'd felt justified at the time. He'd been surprised when Sophie had first contacted him, telling him that their last time together before their breakup had resulted in pregnancy, but he'd been willing to take responsibility. Clearly there was no room in his life for a baby just then, but he could help financially and figure out a way to be a part of his child's life.

He'd been thrown when Sophie had insisted that money was all he'd need to provide. But then he'd learned that she'd found a new boyfriend and had told *him* that he was the baby's father. Furious at the way she'd tried to use him, Seth had cut off all communication with Sophie, until that day in Key West. It wasn't until he became a Christian that Seth realized how badly he'd behaved then, and how he'd let his anger push him to act so disdainfully in dismissing Sophie and Olivia. Now he had to pray that Elise would believe he'd changed.

"Thanks for coming."

"I can't stay long." She took another step closer. "You were in surgery a long time. Nearly four hours. Dad told us how they had to cut you out of the car." Elise swallowed hard.

Seth wished he knew what she was thinking, but maybe he didn't want to know. "Your dad helped me hang on. I don't remember much except your dad praying."

"I'm so sorry you had this accident, but I'm glad he could help." Elise crossed her arms over her midsection, appearing ill at ease again.

"Did you see Olivia?"

Elise nodded. "She's with your mom now, but she was asking for you."

"I wish I could see her, but it probably wouldn't be a very good idea right now." Seth's heart swelled with love for his little girl. He wondered whether Elise could ever share that feeling.

"I think you're right. You're kind of banged up."

Seth smiled wryly. "Thanks."

Elise hunched her shoulders. "I didn't mean to insult you."

Seth couldn't help laughing even though it hurt. "No insult taken."

"Guess I'd better leave, so you can get some rest." She turned to go.

Seth tried to sit up, but he barely had the strength. He didn't want her to go. If only she would stay. If only she could care for him again. "Elise…"

Stopping, she turned back. "I hope you recover soon. I'll be praying for you."

He watched her walk away without a backward glance.

Shutting his eyes, Seth sagged back against the pillow. The sound of Elise's heels clicking on the tile floor still echoed in his head. Each click had pounded home her goodbye. She hadn't said one word about seeing him again. The accident may not have killed him, but it had certainly killed his plans to win back Elise's heart. Unless she was willing to visit him, he had no chance to see her when he was stuck in a hospital bed.

In the days that followed, Elise used work and school to avoid visiting Seth again. She was a coward and couldn't bring herself to go into the ICU.

Elise slammed her book closed and walked to the window that overlooked the front yard. As she took in the sunny day, her mother's car pulled to a stop at the curb in front of the house.

Elise watched as her mother, Maggie and Olivia got out of the car and came up the walk toward the front door. Elise's stomach churned. Why couldn't they have waited fifteen minutes to show up? Juliane would've been home by then and could greet the company. Elise had to answer the door instead of remaining upstairs out of sight.

The doorbell rang before Elise reached the bottom of the stairs. She took a deep breath and pasted a smile on her face as she opened the door.

"Hi, dear. Having a good day?" Without waiting for an answer, Barbara marched into the living room, then motioned for Maggie and Olivia to join her.

"I've been studying. I have a big paper to write for one of my classes." Elise turned to Maggie. "How's Seth?"

"Doing better. They moved him out of ICU and into a regular room today."

"That's good to hear."

"We took Olivia to see him for the first time." Maggie glanced down at her granddaughter.

"Hi, 'Lise." Olivia reached out and pulled on Elise's pant leg. "Daddy hurt."

"I know." Elise hunkered down next to Olivia. "I've been praying for your daddy. I'm glad he's getting better."

Barbara tapped Elise's shoulder. "We came over to find out whether you'd be able to watch Olivia on Friday while Seth's belongings are unloaded from the moving van. Since you don't have class on Friday, I thought you could help."

Standing, Elise saw a test in her mother's request. Now Elise knew why her mother had stopped by rather than calling. With Maggie and Olivia standing there, how could Elise refuse to watch the little girl? She felt the pressure to comply, drawing her back into Seth's life. "I should be able to do that."

Maggie's expression was painted with relief. "Thank you.

Thank you. Having you watch her will make the move so much easier."

"I'm glad to help." Even as Elise said it she realized she meant it. Despite everything, she wanted to help.

"Wonderful!" Barbara clasped her hands. "That'll work for this week. I'm working on a plan for us to watch Olivia once Maggie returns home."

"When will that be?" Elise took in the conversation with growing dread. What was her mother thinking? Fearing the direction in which this conversation appeared to be heading, Elise wished she could somehow send her mother a mental message.

"Unless Seth takes a turn for the worse, which is unlikely now, I have to be back to work on Monday."

"We'll take care of Olivia, won't we?" Barbara turned to Elise.

Before Elise could formulate her reply, Maggie eyed Elise. "Could we talk?"

Swallowing hard, Elise wasn't sure what to think of Maggie's question. Did it have to do with watching Olivia or something else? "Sure."

Barbara took Olivia's hand. "While you two talk, Olivia and I'll see about finding something to entertain us."

Elise watched her mother and Olivia disappear down the hallway toward Juliane's office. Did her mother know what Maggie intended to say? Was that why her mother was leaving—to give them some privacy? "What did you want to talk about?"

Maggie licked her lips, then took a deep breath. "I know you and Seth didn't part on the best of terms, but he wants to make things right between you."

Elise didn't know how to take Maggie's statement. How did Seth want to make things right?

Maggie didn't wait for Elise to respond. "Please give Seth a chance to talk with you."

"Today?"

"I know he'd like that."

"Is he up to it? He was pretty groggy when I saw him the last time."

"He asked for you."

Elise didn't know how to react. Mixed feelings about Seth charged into her thoughts. Part of her wanted to find an excuse not to see him, but the other part knew she had to give him a chance. The pressure to deal with him was coming at her from all quarters, and she couldn't make excuses to avoid him any longer. Besides, maybe Juliane was right. Maybe this was what she needed to finally put the whole mess behind her. "I'll try my best to find time to see him."

Maggie touched Elise's arm. "I understand this can't be easy, so I appreciate it."

Elise couldn't fault Maggie's concern for her son, and she seemed to understand any reticence Elise might feel about the visit. "Thanks for understanding."

Olivia ran back into the room as she waved a piece of paper over her head. "Gramma, see my picture?"

"Very nice." Smiling, Maggie patted Olivia on the top of the head. "Tell me about your drawing."

"That's Daddy." Olivia held up her coloring sheet higher so Elise could see.

"That's very colorful." Elise glanced at the paper covered with a swirl of scribbles that looked nothing like a human, but the jumble of lines must have said "Daddy" to Olivia.

"You take it." Smiling, Olivia held up the paper.

"Thanks." Reaching it, Elise noticed for the first time how Olivia's little smile reminded her of Seth's—the smile that used to make her heart trip. A gamut of emotions inundated her as she held the crisp paper.

Barbara glanced at Elise. "You should put Olivia's drawing on your refrigerator."

Elise smiled at her mother. "Okay."

As Elise entered the kitchen, Juliane walked in from the garage. Elise slapped the picture on the refrigerator with a magnet advertising Keller's Variety, the family department store. "Hi, Juliane. We have company."

"So I see." Juliane plunked her purse and satchel on the kitchen table. "You don't seem very happy about it."

Elise nodded toward the living room. "I'll fill you in after they leave."

"Okay." Juliane headed into the living room.

Elise followed Juliane and stood off to the side as Juliane greeted their mother, Maggie and Olivia. After a few minutes of conversation that included filling in Juliane about the plans for watching Olivia, the visitors left.

After the door closed, Juliane turned to Elise. "I see what has you a little unhappy."

"The plans for watching Olivia are only part of it." Shaking her head, Elise sighed. "Seth's mother asked me to visit with him because he wants to talk with me. Something about making things right between us."

Juliane nodded and gave Elise a knowing look. "I'm in complete agreement. It's time to deal with Seth. Get the talk over with, and after that, if you want to keep your distance, at least you've gotten the discussion out of the way."

Elise didn't want to admit that her sister was right, but she was. "Okay. I might as well get it over with. I'm going to go up to the hospital after we eat supper. Will you go with me?"

"How are you going to talk to him if I'm there?"

"I just need your support when we first get there."

"You mean, after we're there for a few minutes I can make my excuses and leave?"

"Yeah. That's kind of what I had in mind." Elise made

her way into the kitchen to start cooking supper. While she worked, she tried to figure out what she was going to say to Seth. One thing topped the list. Why did he now have custody of Olivia?

Chapter Five

Elise hoped the beauty of the setting sun that painted the sky in red and gold was a good sign for this visit with Seth. Taking a deep breath in an effort to calm her herself, she walked into the hospital, holding the door open for Juliane.

"Are you sure you're going to be okay with this?" her sister asked. "You've never been very good with blood and stuff like that. I don't want you fainting on me."

Elise let out a long harsh breath. Lifting her chin, she squared her shoulders. "I'm not going to faint. Remember, I saw his injuries before."

"Okay, then. Let's go." Juliane strode toward the reception desk.

"We're here to see Seth Finley. Can you tell us what room he's in?" Elise held her breath as she waited.

"Let me see." The bespectacled woman turned to her computer screen.

The beat of Elise's heart matched the *clack, clack, clack* of the keyboard as the woman typed.

The woman looked up from her computer screen. "He's in room two fourteen."

"Thanks." Elise headed to the elevators.

While Elise and Juliane rode to the second floor in silence, Elise tried to figure out what she would say to Seth. Maybe all she had to do was listen. Would he have an excuse for what he had done?

As the elevator doors opened, Juliane glanced at Elise. "Are you ready?"

Elise nodded. "This isn't going to be easy, but I'm ready."

"Good." Juliane pointed down the hall. "Room two fourteen is that way."

"Okay." Elise followed, taking in the medicinal smell and the beeping machines. "Thanks for coming with me."

"Glad to help."

Elise said a prayer as a new sense of dread that hadn't been there just seconds before inundated her mind. But she could do this. Slowly, she put one foot in front of the other as they passed the bank of monitors along the wall in the nurses' station.

As they drew near the room, Dr. Daubenmire came out, followed by a nurse. He glanced up from the chart he carried. "Elise. Juliane. Are you here to visit Seth?"

Elise nodded. "Is he doing okay? Can he have visitors?"

Dr. Daubenmire nodded. "You can visit, but he's still in quite a lot of discomfort. The pain medication may make him somewhat incoherent."

"Thanks, Dr. Daubenmire." Elise wondered whether Seth would be able to carry on a conversation.

"Are you ready?" Juliane's question stopped Elise's speculation.

Elise turned. "I am."

"Good. Let's go." Without waiting for Elise, Juliane charged into Seth's room.

Summoning her courage, Elise hurried after Juliane. Elise surveyed the room. Eyes closed, Seth lay on the bed, one leg elevated and encased in a cast. Bandages peeked out from under the hospital gown that fit loosely across his torso. Machines and wires surrounded him. As she observed the red mark across his forehead that contrasted with the paleness of the rest of his face, a huge hand seemed to be pressing down on her chest.

Elise stepped closer to Juliane and whispered, "Do you think he's sleeping?"

Juliane shrugged.

Elise gazed at Seth's face. Even with his injuries, he was handsome. Her heart did a little flip-flop as she watched him. How could she let that happen? She'd spent months telling herself that she was over him, that she couldn't care about someone who had clearly never cared for her. So how could she still respond just to the sight of him, even after all her prayers to take her feelings for him away? Her prayer hadn't been answered…or had it?

How did God want her to deal with Seth?

The question zipped through her mind while she thought of the changes she'd made in her life since returning home. She was finally feeling settled and working to keep her life in tune with God. Would Seth throw all of that out of whack? Or was his return into her life part of a higher plan?

Elise placed one hand over her heart and leaned toward the bed. "Seth."

His eyes flickered open. He seemed to be trying to focus. Then he smiled. "Elise? You're actually here. Or am I dreaming?"

She swallowed a lump in her throat. He didn't seem to remember she'd come to see him while he'd been in the ICU. Everything in her wanted to reach out and take his hand, but she feared her own reaction and what it might mean.

Despite her questions, Elise knew she couldn't let him draw her in. No matter what his role was meant to be in her life, for her own peace of mind she had to remain aloof—detached. It hurt too much to even think of caring for him again. She wanted him to get better, but she couldn't get involved in his life.

"You aren't imagining." She forced herself to remain calm even though her insides were scrambled. "How are you doing?"

"I'm alive. That about says it." His eyes drifted shut. "I'm feeling…well…a little drowsy."

"Do you want us to leave?"

His eyes fluttered open. "No. Stay."

The weariness in his voice made her want to comfort him. She pushed back the urge. "You do sound tired. So we won't stay long."

"I'm dopey from the painkillers." He smiled weakly. "Have a seat."

"I'll stand." Elise resisted his request out of self-preservation. "So you're feeling better?"

Seth nodded. "You two still don't look like sisters."

Although his statement was true, Elise thought it came out of the blue. Figuring the drugs were talking, she ignored the comment. "I'm glad you're doing well."

"I wouldn't say 'well' exactly. I've got a long road of recovery ahead. But considering the alternative, I'm certainly grateful."

Juliane stepped closer to the bed. "You're lucky to be alive."

Seth touched his forehead. "Yeah, this big red mark is from the airbag, which definitely saved my life."

Elise swallowed the lump that formed in her throat as Seth explained only one of his injuries. "The airbag did that?"

He nodded, then touched his shoulder. "And the seat belt, another lifesaver, tore up my shoulder, but I'm here."

Elise didn't want to think about how close Seth had probably come to death. "Any idea how long before you get out of the hospital?"

"No. Broken leg, broken ribs, internal bleeding. They patched me up, but no telling when they'll let me out." Seth gave her a weak smile. "Your dad saved my life. I don't know how I can ever thank him."

Elise didn't know what to say as another lump rose in her throat. An image of the accident flitted through her mind. Pushing it away, she tried to focus on the thought of her dad's calming voice, not his description of Seth's car wrapped around a tree. "Dad was glad he came back to find you."

"Me, too." Seth closed his eyes, his voice sounding tired again.

"Are you sure you're up for company?" Elise's gaze traveled to Seth's face.

"Yeah. Please stay." Opening his eyes, Seth tried to sit up. "We haven't had a chance to talk yet."

"But you seem tired."

"I'm fine."

Before Elise could say another word, a nurse, sporting a colorful smock, bustled into the room and looked at Elise and Juliane. "You'll need to leave the room for a few minutes. As soon as I'm done, you can come right back."

"Are you here again?" Seth grinned. "You just can't live without me."

"I know." The nurse chuckled. "I have to keep checking those vital signs. We don't want you expiring on us."

Elise took in their exchange. Nothing much had changed about Seth. Even lying in a hospital bed, he was charming the women. Clearly the end of their relationship hadn't left him too broken up. He certainly hadn't forgotten how to flirt. Well, she wouldn't worry about it. She'd listen to what he had to say, and that would be the end of it. He might be here in town, but she was determined to lead her own life, and he could lead his.

"Okay." Without glancing his way, Elise motioned to Juliane and headed for the door.

"Elise?"

She turned as she reached the door. "Yes?"

"You're coming back, right?"

"As long as the nurse says it's okay."

The nurse smiled. "Absolutely. You can come back in as soon as I'm done."

With Juliane close behind, Elise stepped into the hall and leaned against the wall.

Joining her, Juliane touched her arm. "Are you okay?"

"I'm good. If you want to go, you can."

"Are you sure?"

Elise nodded. "I can deal with it."

"Okay, but you want me to call you on your cell in a little while in case you need an excuse to leave?"

Elise chuckled. "No, I can make my own excuse."

"You're sounding a little more in control."

"Not me so much, but I'm trying to let God be in control."

"Good thinking. I'll see you later." Juliane gave Elise a hug. "You can fill me in when you get home. I'm going to stop and see Lukas on the way. I've got some wedding stuff to run by him."

"Does he really care?"

Juliane gave Elise an impish grin. "Probably not, but I want him to feel like he's involved."

"Have fun." Elise motioned for Juliane to go. "Talk to you later.

While Elise waited, questions buzzed through her mind. How would God use this reunion with Seth? What was God trying to teach her?

She couldn't help thinking about Juliane's relationship with Lukas. They had known each other in college, but Lukas's alcohol addiction at the time had led to behavior Juliane had found very hard to forgive. It had taken time for him to prove to her that he'd changed, but eventually they'd let go of the past and had fallen in love. Now this accident was making her face the stuff about Seth she'd conveniently pushed to the dark recesses of her mind.

These unforeseen circumstances had changed everything and forced her to face Seth and the past. Had he changed, as well? It seemed unlikely, but how could she be sure? Talking things out was the only way to know.

Could she face Seth alone? She'd leaned on Juliane earlier, but now she had to stand on her own. What was Seth going to tell her? Was she ready to hear his story?

When Elise reentered the room, Seth breathed a sigh of relief. She'd actually stayed, and Juliane wasn't with her. That would give him a better opportunity to explain his life in the past year and a half to Elise.

"Juliane couldn't stay. She had to go meet Lukas." Elise stepped closer to the bed, but she still appeared tense and wary, staring at him with those brandy-colored eyes. They made him remember the love that used to radiate from them. Could that ever happen again?

"I'm glad *you* could stay."

Elise looked as if she wanted to bolt. "If you're not up to visiting tonight, I can come another time. Your mom told me you were ready for visitors. She wanted me to talk to you."

"I'm fine." Seth's heart took a nosedive. Elise wasn't here because she wanted to see him. She was here again because his mother had probably badgered her into coming.

"You're sure?" As Elise gazed at him, the golden highlights in her brown hair shimmered in the overhead lights.

Seth nodded, knowing no matter how he felt he had to take advantage of her presence now. So he'd better start talking, or Elise would probably decide to leave. "If you don't mind, could you please bring the chair closer to the bed and sit down?"

"Sure." She pushed the chair toward the head of the bed and placed it so she was facing him. Looking like a child who had been called into the principal's office, she sat straight-backed with her hands folded in her lap.

Seth wanted to tell her to relax, but that wouldn't get them off to a very good start. The tension in her shoulders told him that she wasn't eager to be here. He wished he could make her feel more at ease. How was he going to start this conversation?

He needed to collect his thoughts, not an easy task considering the pain medication. He might as well get right to the point. "I suppose you're wondering how I came to have Olivia. I guess I should start there."

Wide-eyed, she nodded. "That would be good."

Telling Elise about Olivia had been his idea, but now that he had a chance to explain, his mind was numb. The words wouldn't form in his mouth. "I've changed."

"How?" Her skeptical tone stabbed him in the heart.

"I know I said I'd start with Olivia, but I have to tell you what came before in order for it all to make sense."

"Go ahead. I'm here to listen." Nothing in Elise's expression changed.

Seth's heart sank when she crossed her arms—a sure sign she didn't want to be here. Convincing her that he was different wouldn't be easy. "The day we saw Sophie with Olivia, I was very angry. She'd lied to me the last time we'd spoken."

"What lies?" Elise's inflection and unchanging demeanor made her continued skepticism very evident.

Pain that the medication couldn't blunt surrounded his heart as he told Elise about Sophie's deceptions. "She was string-ing me and her current boyfriend both along so she could get twice as much money. Once I found that out, I cut all ties. I convinced myself that Olivia wasn't mine at all and refused to even have a paternity test. Looking back now, I can see how wrong I was, how I punished an innocent baby for her mother's mistake. But I was too angry to see that at the time. Then everything changed."

"How?" This time genuine interest sounded in Elise's ques-tion as she dropped her arms.

Elise's response filled Seth with hope that she would finally understand the reasons for what he'd done. "I told you about my dad's sudden death the other night. His death caused me to examine my life. At the funeral, I saw the influence he had had on the people who knew him. I vowed then and there to be a man like my dad."

Nodding, Elise leaned forward. "I remember your dad from when your parents came on one of our cruises. He impressed me as the kind of man you describe."

Taking in Elise's statement, Seth didn't say anything for a moment. She was probably comparing him to his father and thinking he didn't measure up. "My dad was definitely someone to look up to, but he didn't take credit for himself. He gave God the credit."

"A good thing to do."

"Before my father's death, I didn't have much use for God. You were aware of that."

Elise nodded, sorrow in her eyes. "You made that pretty clear."

Seth sighed. "Yeah. I thought my parents and their religion were old-fashioned. Who needed God?"

"So you're saying you changed your mind when your father died?"

"His death made me think about my own life. I started

attending church with my mother, because it was important to her. I wanted to do whatever I could to help her with her grief. And in the process, and much to my surprise, I became a believer."

"I'm glad to hear that." She stood and turned toward the window, refusing to look at him. "Now tell me about Olivia."

Seth sensed Elise's withdrawal as she gazed out the window. "Is everything all right?"

"Yes. Just get on with your story."

"Please sit down again."

Turning to look at him, she shrugged. "If that's what you want."

"I do."

"I'm listening." She sat, her posture tense again.

"When I became a Christian, I realized I'd lived a very self-centered life." Seth tried to gauge Elise's reaction to his statement, but she appeared unmoved. He wasn't sure what to make of her lack of response. "I knew I had to try to make amends. To forgive those who had wronged me and seek forgiveness from the people I'd treated badly in return. Especially you and Sophie. I needed to let her know that I'd forgiven her for her deception. I also wanted to find out if I really was a father. I'd refused to even consider the idea before, but once I let go of my anger, I realized there was a real chance that I was Olivia's father. I tried to contact both of you."

"So that's why you've been calling me?"

"Yes." *But you wouldn't talk to me.* He wanted to say that, but right now those words would probably only alienate her further.

Tears welled in her eyes as she waved her hand toward him. "I'm sorry I wouldn't talk to you before. Can you forgive me?"

"Do you think we can forgive each other?"

Elise didn't say anything for what seemed like forever. She blinked back the tears and released a heavy sigh, then nodded.

"Thanks."

"So that's how you came to have Olivia."

"Not quite. That's just how I started looking for her."

"Was Sophie still in Key West?"

Seth shook his head. "She wasn't there, and no one I talked to seemed to know where she'd gone."

"So what did you do then?"

"A couple of people suggested she might have gone back to Atlanta, where she'd lived before."

"Was she there?"

"No."

"How did you find her?"

"I didn't."

"Then how—"

"How did I get Olivia?"

Elise nodded.

Seth took a deep breath. "I received a call saying Sophie intended to give Olivia up for adoption."

"Why?" Shock sounded in Elise's voice.

"I'm not sure." Seth stared at his cast, breaking eye contact with Elise. He didn't want to see her reaction to what he was about to say. She didn't think much of him. She'd made that quite clear when she ended their relationship. His own guilt over the situation didn't help. Would the rest of the story change her mind or only confirm what she already believed about him?

"What did the caller say?"

"The woman only mentioned the adoption and that I was listed as the father on the birth certificate."

"So you didn't know anything about Sophie's frame of mind?"

Seth still couldn't bring himself to look at Elise. He didn't want to tell this part of the story, but he had to be honest with her. "Not at that time, but she'd told me during our confrontation in Key West that she was thinking about giving up Olivia for adoption. I didn't care then, because I didn't think she was mine."

"What did you do?"

"I immediately took a paternity test, which proved I was Olivia's father just as Sophie had said. I'd done nothing to help her, and I knew that was a terrible mistake."

"Did you talk to Sophie?"

Finally looking at Elise again, Seth shook his head. "I didn't have any contact with her. I tried, but everything was done through a third party, so I never had the chance to say I was sorry. I guess she didn't want anything to do with me."

"Does she know you have Olivia?"

Seth shrugged. "All I know is she signed away her parental rights, and I got custody."

"Why didn't she come after you again for child support?"

"I have no idea." Seth hated that he'd refused to help Sophie when she'd asked. He'd only been thinking of his anger. He'd wanted to hurt her, as she'd hurt him with her deception, and he hadn't given a second thought to the blameless child trapped between them. Elise had been right to disapprove of his behavior. But what did that mean for them now? Would she always see him as the guy who'd refused to help his own child and her mother—the guy whose actions caused a little girl's mother to give up her parental rights? Could he ever live that down?

"Don't you wonder what happened to Sophie?"

Seth swallowed hard. That was a loaded question. Elise was obviously wondering what had happened to Sophie. He'd respected her wishes not to contact her, but sometimes he wondered if his actions were driven by something other than respect, because remembering her put his guilt front and center. The pain in his heart over the situation matched the pain in his body.

When he didn't answer immediately, Elise stood. "Are you getting tired? Maybe I should go now."

"Please don't." Seth reached out his hand but let it fall to his side when Elise backed away. His heart crumbled.

"I've been praying for Sophie. I know that doesn't do away with the awful way I treated her, but I never had a chance to ask for her forgiveness." Seth held Elise's gaze. "But I'm glad I have the chance to tell you I'm sorry for the way I acted."

"I'll pray for Sophie, too." Surprise painted Elise's expression. "And I'm glad we've had this chance to talk. I accept your apology."

"I appreciate that." Seth said a silent prayer of thanksgiving that Elise had accepted his apology and that they'd found common ground on at least one thing—prayers for Sophie.

"I really do have to go now." Elise stood and started for the door.

"Thanks for coming. Good night." Seth wanted to ask whether she planned to visit again, but he didn't want to sound too needy, even though he was right now. He watched her leave the room again without a backward glance. Did he have any hope that she saw him in a different light? He had to learn to leave those kinds of questions in God's hands.

Chapter Six

❧

The early-morning sun glinted off the windshield of the multicolored moving van. It lumbered to a stop along the curb in front of the white clapboard house trimmed with black shutters where Seth would eventually live. Red and yellow tulips displayed their vivid blooms in front yards all along the quiet street a few blocks from the center of town.

Elise parked her car across the street and hurried to the front door. When she stepped onto the porch that went across the entire front of the house, Maggie opened the door, and Olivia ran out. "Hi, 'Lise."

"Hi, Olivia. How are you this morning?"

Giggling, she raced back and forth across the porch. As she made another pass, Elise grabbed the little girl and picked her up. The child giggled again. The sound warmed Elise's heart.

"Good morning. Olivia is going to keep you on your toes today. She is full of extra energy." Maggie motioned for Elise to come in. "The moving van is on time, and God has provided us with a perfect day for moving Seth's things, hasn't He?"

"Absolutely." Stepping inside, Elise realized she should

have Maggie's attitude. Elise needed God's sunshine in her soul, as well as the sunshine outside.

Elise surveyed the inside of the house as she set Olivia down. The child scampered to the coloring book she'd spread on the dark hardwood floor, picked it up and raced back to Elise, her little footsteps echoing through the empty living room. "Look."

"What do you have here?" Elise gazed at the child. Her sweet little face reminded her of Seth's earnest expression when he'd confessed to her. His story had caught her off guard, putting a whole new slant on his behavior. He'd still done wrong, but she understood his actions better now. She'd told the truth when she'd said she'd forgiven him. But where did that leave them? Forgiveness couldn't erase the memory of the fight they'd had over Sophie, or the way it had made her question everything they'd shared.

So what now? She couldn't help remembering Seth's statement about God using even the bad stuff in our lives. Did Seth believe his accident had brought with it the chance for them to reconcile? Was that even what he wanted, or was her forgiveness his only goal?

Elise shook away all the questions as Olivia shoved the coloring book at her. "See my picture?"

"Very nice."

"For my daddy." Her expression filled with concern. "My daddy's hurt."

Again, the child's expression touched Elise. Hoping to waylay Olivia's fears, Elise hunkered down next to the little girl. "I visited your daddy in the hospital the other day. He's doing much better."

"I love my daddy."

Me, too. The words popped into Elise's head. The unexpected thought froze her brain for a moment. She shook the words away before they could settle in her mind. They weren't true. They were far from the truth. Any love she had for Seth was in the past—dead and gone. She'd moved on...hadn't she?

Did it matter that he'd changed? Did it matter that he'd asked for forgiveness and displayed a completely different attitude? That was what scared her. These changes were breaking down her resistance to his charm. She'd felt her resolve to keep her distance crumbling while she'd stood next to his hospital bed. When he'd reached out to her, she'd almost taken his hand. Just in time, she'd backed away.

She could forgive him. She could help him with Olivia. She could help him find a place in the community, but she couldn't go as far as being a close friend. For her own peace of mind, she should keep her distance. She'd fooled herself once into believing that he loved her and that they could be happy together, but she wouldn't let herself be fooled again.

Olivia tugged on Elise's pant leg and brought her thoughts to an abrupt end. "Be my friend?"

Elise's heart turned over as she read the expectation in Olivia's eyes. The question buzzed through Elise's mind. Would being a friend to Olivia mean being friends with her father? Was Olivia's request God's way of showing Elise what to do? She didn't know the answer, but she couldn't deny the little girl's request. "Okay. We can be friends."

Twirling around the room, Olivia clapped her hands.

While Elise watched with amusement, her mother and several women from the Ladies' Circle at church arrived. After Maggie opened the door, the women scurried inside, all of them talking and laughing at once as they exclaimed over Olivia. The little girl drank up the attention.

Olivia entertained the ladies, and Maggie talked with the movers. Elise continued to watch the little girl, who was a charmer just like her father. Elise wondered whether she would always see Seth when she looked at Olivia.

Barbara stepped away from the group of ladies and joined Elise. "You should walk to the park so Olivia can play. Then you can go up to the hospital and visit Seth."

Elise's stomach sank at her mother's second suggestion. *Are you trying to run my life?* The question sat on the tip of Elise's tongue, but she pressed her lips together in an effort not to voice it. Her mother meant well. "I suppose it would be a good idea to get her out of the way while the movers and all of you ladies are working."

Barbara nodded. "And I know she'd like to visit her daddy."

"I'll play it by ear." Was her mother trying to push Seth and her together? Elise tried to erase the speculation from her thoughts. Her own worries about Seth were making her paranoid.

Although Elise hadn't visited Seth again after their talk, she knew she had to work at keeping her promise to forgive him. And that meant she couldn't always avoid him. Seth was making an effort to lead a different life. He'd become a Christian, and she needed to treat him as a brother in the Lord. That was the hardest part. Could she love him like a brother without letting old feelings creep into her thoughts? Despite the changes he'd made in his life, she didn't even want to entertain the idea of a relationship with him. They couldn't go back. It wouldn't work.

"How's our patient this morning?" Dr. Daubenmire stopped at the foot of the bed and studied the medical chart.

"I'd be a whole lot better if those nurses would let me sleep." Seth pressed the control on his bed to make it rise to a sitting position. "Hospital life has begun to weigh on me. I think those nurses are trying to kill me rather than heal me."

Dr. Daubenmire smiled. "What would you say if I told you

that we're releasing you tomorrow? I've consulted with Dr. Bryant, and he agrees."

"Are you serious?" Seth couldn't help grinning. "You mean, I get to go home?"

"I didn't say you get to go home. I'm releasing you to the nursing home."

Seth frowned. "Nursing home? Isn't that for old people?"

The doctor chuckled. "You're going to need rehab. That's a great place to get it."

Just as Seth was about to protest, Elise appeared in the doorway, holding Olivia's hand and carrying a vase of flowers. "May we come in, or should we wait?"

Seth's pulse quickened at the sight of Elise and his daughter standing together. They looked so right, but he couldn't let his mind go there. His heart was jumping too far ahead of reality. He still needed to gain Elise's trust before he could ever think about them reuniting as a couple. He hoped they could fall in love again, but he had to be patient.

Dr. Daubenmire stepped away from the bed. "Come right in. I was just leaving."

"Hi, Daddy." Olivia raced into the room, then pointed to Elise. "See what we bringed you?"

"Hi, sweetheart." Seth heart turned to mush every time he heard that little voice calling him Daddy. And to think he'd almost refused to be part of her life. He couldn't imagine that now. "What did you bring me?"

"Flowers. You like?"

Elise placed the vase on the bedside table, then looked at Dr. Daubenmire. "How's the patient?"

"Doing great." The doctor turned toward the door. "I've got other patients to see, so I'll let Seth tell you his good news."

"Good news?" Elise picked up Olivia and stepped closer to the bed but kept her gaze focused on Olivia.

"I'm getting out of here tomorrow."

"Did you hear that, Olivia? Your daddy gets out of the hospital tomorrow."

"Daddy come home?"

Seth sighed. "Well, not exactly."

Elise finally turned his way, a little frown puckering her brow. "What do you mean, not exactly?"

"Doc says I have to go to the nursing home for rehab."

Grinning, Elise set Olivia on the edge of the bed. "I know that probably sounds crazy to you, but they have the best rehab facility in town. One of my cousins is a physical therapist there. They're all fantastic. Besides, you wouldn't be able to take care of yourself or Olivia at home."

"True." Seth reached over and gave Olivia a hug with one arm. "Where did you get the flowers?"

"I picked them."

Seth glanced up at Elise. "She did?"

Elise gave him a lopsided grin. "Tulips and lilacs from your yard."

"You've been to my house?"

"They're moving your stuff in today, or did you forget?"

"Oh, yeah, this is Friday." Seth leaned back in the bed. "Mom mentioned that yesterday. All the days and nights seem to flow together in here."

"They're making terrific progress. Your mom has everything under control. With your mom, my mom and the other ladies from church putting things away, you'll have the neatest house in town."

"Yeah. Until I move into it." Chuckling, Seth gazed at Olivia. "Have you been a good girl for Grandma?"

Olivia nodded her head, her curls bobbing. "Yes."

"I'm glad to hear that." Seth glanced up at Elise to see her reaction to Olivia's pronouncement.

"Olivia has been very busy today, haven't you?" Elise looked down at his daughter.

"'Lise taked me to the park."

"Did you have fun?"

"I swinged and slided on the slide."

"Great!" Seth patted Olivia on the head.

"Are you going to show your daddy what you made him?"

Nodding, Olivia fished an envelope from the pocket of her jacket and handed it to Seth. "For you."

"Thank you. It's very nice." Seth examined the envelope decorated with a big red heart and the words "I love you" printed in neat block letters. He knew Olivia hadn't written the words or made the heart. Was this his mother's work or Elise's? It was silly to speculate. Even if Elise had written the words, they were Olivia's feelings, not Elise's.

"'Lise drew the heart." Olivia patted the carefully drawn heart. "See inside."

"Okay." Seth ripped open the envelope. Inside he found a folded piece of paper. He unfolded it and surveyed the picture of a teddy bear colored pink as only a two-and-a-half-year-old could color. "You did this all by yourself?"

Olivia nodded. "Pink."

"That's right. Pink it is. You did a great job." Seth gave Olivia another hug, then turned his attention to Elise. "What else did you do today?"

"All the ladies and Olivia and I had lunch at my cousin's café."

"That's where I was supposed to have breakfast the morning of the accident. How about going there with me to celebrate my getting sprung from this place?" Seth waved a hand around the room, then realized what he'd done when he saw Elise's wary expression. He'd practically asked her for a date. Would including Olivia ease Elise's unease? "I'm sure Olivia would like to go again, wouldn't you?"

Elise's expression didn't change as she smiled at Olivia,

not at him. "I'm sure she would, but I hardly think you'll be able to go to the café to eat until after you go through your rehab."

"Really?"

"Really. Surely Dr. Daubenmire has explained everything to you."

Seth gazed out the window. Yeah. The doctor had gone over the timeline for recovery, but Seth had somehow figured it wouldn't be like that for him. He'd beat the odds and be on his feet in no time. He had a new job to start and a little girl to take care of. How was he going to do all that and rehab, too? Getting out of the hospital was only the first step in a long recovery. "He did, but—"

"But you thought somehow all that stuff wasn't going to apply to you, right?"

Shaking his head, Seth couldn't help smiling. Elise had nearly spoken his thoughts. "How did you know?"

"Because I know you."

She knows me. The thought rattled around in his head. She knew the old Seth, not the new one. He had to make her see the new-and-improved version of Seth Finley. Each encounter with her reaffirmed his feelings. He was still in love with Elise Keller. She'd captured his heart on the high seas, and when she'd walked out of his life, she'd taken his heart with her. Nothing he'd said or done at the time had been enough to change her mind. Then going home to help his mother had left him without another chance to persuade her to take him back. Though he couldn't fault her for walking away, he couldn't stop wanting her back. What were the chances he could win her heart again?

Did he dare dispute her assessment? "You think you know me, but I think I'll surprise you."

"We'll see." She gave him a pensive look as she rummaged in her satchel and brought out a coloring book and crayons.

"Olivia, would you like to color another picture for your daddy?"

Olivia nodded as Elise pushed the tray table up next to the bed so the little girl could use it as a desk. Elise laid several crayons on the table next to the open coloring book. Olivia immediately picked up the pink crayon and began to scribble on the picture of a tree. A pink tree. Seth smiled.

"Hey, everyone." Barbara waltzed into the room.

"Mom, what are you doing here?"

"Just stopped by to let Seth know the movers have finished and all his possessions are now in his new house." Barbara stood at the end of the bed. "Your mother has everything under control."

"I had no doubt she would." Seth chuckled, knowing that while sometimes he chafed under his mother's advice, she always had good intentions. "She likes to have everything under control."

Barbara sighed. "Well, there's one thing she doesn't have under control. I think she's worried about what'll happen with Olivia after she leaves."

Seth fought to keep his irritation from showing. Getting annoyed wasn't going to help his cause with Elise. Did his mother think he wasn't capable of caring for his own child?

"I'm not sure why she's worried. As soon as I knew I had this job, I made arrangements for Olivia to be in the day-care center that Ray told me is run by the church." Seth glanced from Elise to Barbara. "And thanks to your plan, someone will be there to take care of her in the evenings until I can finally go home. Mom knows this. So why is she worried?"

"I think she wishes she could be here to help." Barbara moved toward the head of the bed, her gaze holding a hint of sympathy.

Seth sighed again. "I hate that I have to depend on so many people."

Barbara shook her head. "You shouldn't worry about that. We are all here to help. You just need to think about getting well."

"My mom's right, you know. We're here to help, especially with this cutie." Elise tickled Olivia ribs, and she giggled.

Seth's heart felt as though it were beating outside his body. So much emotion was tied up in Olivia and Elise. He was thankful that, for once, a nurse wasn't lurking outside the door ready to take his pulse. The reading might be off the charts.

Waving an index finger in the air, Barbara looked at Seth. "You know…I'm rethinking our plan. I've seen how Olivia seems to have bonded with Elise. I'm thinking Olivia would have a more settled and secure feeling if the same person was there every evening instead of a parade of caregivers." Barbara turned her attention to Elise. "What do you think, dear?"

Seth could read the panic in Elise's eyes. He was sure it had nothing to do with caring for Olivia. It had to do with him. Was she feeling pushed into his life? He didn't want her to feel that way. "I'm sure the original arrangements will work out fine. There's no point in Elise carrying the entire burden."

Elise shook her head as she eyed him. "Seth, my mom's right. It would be better for Olivia to have the same person with her every night."

"And you're willing to do this?"

"I am." Elise looked at Olivia, and love replaced the panic in Elise's eyes.

Swallowing hard, Seth could hardly believe what she'd said, but he wasn't going to question it. Elise was willing to love his little girl and help him, too. That was enough for now.

After taking Maggie to the Cincinnati airport, Elise headed for the nursing home. When Seth had said goodbye to his mother, he'd insisted Elise bring Olivia back to see him before she went to bed. As Elise drove into the parking lot, she had to admit that her former reluctance to visit him had diminished. She wasn't sure when her change of heart had occurred, but it had.

Pink clouds adorned the sky as the setting sun sat just above the trees sporting the first leaves of spring. As Elise helped Olivia out of her car seat, the little girl pointed to the sky. "Pink."

Laughing, Elise picked up Olivia and hugged her. "Yes, the pink sky sure is pretty. You can tell your daddy all about it."

"See Daddy."

"Yes, you get to see your daddy."

Elise opened the door leading into the lobby of the nursing home. The smell of medicine and food from the evening meal filled the air. As she made her way down the hall lined with elderly residents in wheelchairs, Olivia wiggled to get down. Elise set the little girl on the floor. She scampered ahead but stopped before she went into Seth's room.

When Elise reached the doorway, she saw why Olivia had stopped. Seth wasn't there. Instead, a balding older man, who hadn't been in the room when she'd visited earlier, watched TV as he lay in the bed closest to the door. The other bed was empty.

The man glanced their way and smiled. "I guess you're here to see my new roommate?"

"We are." Elise motioned toward the other half of the room. "Do you know where he is?"

The man shrugged. "Can't say for sure, but I'm guessing he's running around on those crutches and flirting with the pretty nurses."

Elise flinched a little at the reminder of Seth's flirtatiousness but quickly reminded herself that it was none of her concern. Instead, she let herself consider the man's friendliness. Was he lonely? "Hope you're doing better, too."

"I'll be better once I get outta here. Mild heart attack. Gotta change my ways." He chuckled. "At least that's what the doc and my wife say."

"It's always good to listen to the doctors and your wife."

"The name is Bud Norman." Chuckling, the man gestured toward Olivia. "And who is this young lady?"

"This is Olivia, Seth's daughter." Elise patted Olivia on the shoulder. "And I'm Elise Keller."

"Hi, Olivia. Hi, Elise."

Elise turned at the sound of Seth's voice. As the little girl raced to greet her daddy, Elise tried to get her wildly racing heart under control. Why had she let her heart fool her again?

But the part of her heart that had never let go of Seth betrayed her as he put aside his crutches and settled in the nearby chair. He picked up Olivia and gathered her into his arms. Elise closed her eyes against the sweet picture. When they were together, she used to wonder what Seth would be like as a father. The reality was better than she'd imagined—except that in this reality, she had no part in the little family.

Why did her feelings about Seth have to be so confusing?

"Elise, are you okay?"

Opening her eyes, she forced herself to smile. "I am."

"Good. For a minute there, I thought maybe you were going to faint."

Laughing halfheartedly, Elise shook her head. "Just gathering my thoughts." *Thoughts about you.*

She had to remember that she and Seth were better off apart. He certainly wasn't pining over her. Bud's comment about Seth's flirting with the nurses proved that. He was acting like the same old Seth she'd known—the charmer who loved to have women eating out of his hand.

Why was she bothered anyway? She had no claims on

Seth, but those old feelings lingered in her heart—feelings that could only lead to hurt if she acted on them. Too many unresolved questions about Seth needed answers before she could even consider giving him access to her heart again.

Chapter Seven

"I've got something in my car that Olivia is going to love." Elise's smile grew into a grin.

"What did you bring her?" Taking in Elise's happiness, Seth maneuvered on his crutches as he followed her down the walk to the driveway where she'd parked her car. Olivia followed close behind him, almost as if she were watching to make sure he would make it down the walk. Although he wasn't as mobile as he'd like to be, he was thankful that after two weeks of rehab in the nursing home he was finally in his own house. Little by little he was getting better. While his body mended, he prayed he could mend his relationship with Elise, as well.

"You'll see in a minute." Elise opened the trunk of her car. "Be careful on those crutches. I don't want to be responsible if you fall down and break something else."

"I'm not going to fall down. This is good for me."

"I suppose, but you make me nervous."

Did that mean she cared about him? He wanted to ask in the worst way, but he didn't dare to put her on the spot. He should just be glad for her help. During the two weeks he'd spent in the nursing home, Elise had taken care of Olivia by spending the night at his house.

Now that he was home, would Elise's visits end? She hadn't said anything about it, and he didn't want to make her feel obligated to help. Even though she'd brought Olivia to the nursing home every evening, he'd sensed the barrier she'd erected—the barrier that clearly indicated she was there for Olivia, not him.

Putting the troubling thoughts from his mind, he hobbled over to the car and looked inside the trunk. A box containing a little wooden kitchen set lay nestled on an old blanket. He glanced at Olivia, then back at Elise. At least if she didn't have much use for him, she obviously cared for his daughter. "Olivia *is* going to love this."

"I'm sorry, but we still have to put it together. It would've been too hard to transport if it was assembled."

"So does that mean you're going to help me?"

Elise chuckled. "I believe you're going to need my help."

"That's a relief." At least it meant she'd be staying awhile.

"What is it?" Standing on her tiptoes, Olivia tried to see into the trunk.

"Step away, sweetheart, so we can get it out." Seth waved her back.

Elise eyed him. "Are you sure you should be helping with this? I got it in the trunk. I should be able to get it out."

"I'm fine." He wanted to give her assistance. He didn't want to feel completely helpless.

Olivia did as he said, standing wide-eyed as he leaned against the car and helped Elise lift the box containing the play kitchen and deposit it on the driveway. Olivia ran and started inspecting the picture on the box. She looked up at Elise. "Mine?"

"Yes, it's your kitchen, but your daddy and I have to put it together. Let me take this inside." Elise reached into the trunk and held up a plastic shopping bag. "I've got pots and pans and little play food items in here, too."

"Play now, please?"

"You can't, honey, not until we take it inside and put it together." Seth gave Elise a helpless look. "Can you manage this by yourself if I open the doors?"

"I think so." Elise handed the bag of food items to Olivia. "You can carry this and help your daddy open the doors for me."

"I help." Olivia scampered ahead, swinging the bag as she went up the walk.

Once inside, Elise set the box in the living room and looked up at Seth. "Is this okay, or do you want to put it together someplace else?"

"Here is fine." Using the box for support, Seth ripped it open and started taking out all of the parts.

Olivia eagerly picked up a couple of the pieces that Seth had laid on the nearby coffee table. Stepping into help, Elise tried to guide Olivia so she wouldn't make a mess. "Olivia, let's put the pieces over here."

After Seth emptied the box, he looked up at Elise. "Do you have any idea where they put my tools when they unpacked?"

Elise shrugged. "Not really, but I'll check in the garage."

Seth's pulse quickened when Elise returned with a large red box containing his tools. He wished he could tell her how he felt, but he was afraid of scaring her away. The fact that Elise cared for his daughter was a good start. He should be satisfied with that for now.

Elise set the tool kit on the floor. Looking at him, she reached for the instructions for assembling the toy kitchen. "I hope this isn't too complicated. I've heard horror stories about putting stuff like this together from my cousins who have kids."

"Me, too, from my mom and dad." Seth couldn't suppress the feelings of hope surrounding his heart because Elise was here. He pointed to the instructions. "I remember them saying to check for all the parts first."

"Good idea."

Olivia stood with her hands on her hips and stared at the two adults. "Me help, too."

"Okay, you can help your daddy keep track of the parts."

Olivia clapped her little hands as she took a seat next to him on the couch. Somehow he'd managed to sit on the couch without falling over. Dealing with the crutches and the plastic cast still wasn't easy. Even though he'd been unhappy in the beginning about going to the nursing home, he was thankful for the time he'd had with the physical therapists there. They'd had him doing gait training with his crutches over even and uneven surfaces and strength training. He still had a long recovery, but they'd given him exercises to help.

For the next two and a half hours, Seth, Elise and even Olivia worked to put the little kitchen together. Still trying not to let his thoughts dwell on his hopes for a new beginning with Elise, Seth took in the camaraderie between Elise and his daughter. He'd been worried that Olivia would always remind Elise of his relationship with Sophie. Seeing Elise and Olivia interact put some of his fear to rest, but he wouldn't know for certain unless he asked Elise directly. Of course, he wasn't going to do that anytime soon. She seemed comfortable and happy in his home for now. He didn't want to bring up an uncomfortable subject and drive her away.

After Seth drilled in the last screw, he set his electric screwdriver aside and looked at Olivia. "It's ready. Do you want to try it out?"

Her curls dancing, Olivia jumped up and down and clapped

her hands. She bounded toward the kitchen and began opening doors and turning knobs again. Then she looked up at Seth. "Cook Daddy food."

Grinning, Seth nodded. Her excitement was contagious. "What are you going to cook for me?"

With her dark eyes wide, Olivia stared at him. For once she didn't have anything to say.

"Do you need pots, pans and food?" Stepping forward, Elise picked up the plastic bag that Olivia had earlier dropped on the floor and forgotten. "Let's look in here. I've got some stuff for your kitchen."

Olivia took the bag from Elise and dumped its contents. Little pots, pans and plastic miniature replicas of meat, fruits and vegetables littered the light brown area rug. The little girl began rummaging through the items as if she'd found great treasures. She held up an apple. "Apple."

"Very good, Olivia. Yes, that's an apple." Elise patted the little girl on the head.

Seemingly pleased with herself for identifying the fruit, she began to name the other pieces of fruit one by one.

Seth hunkered down and picked up some of the toy food and put it on the counter of the little kitchen. "Now you can put everything away, then you can cook something for me."

"'Kay." Olivia started gathering the pretend food and putting it away.

Elise turned to him. "Do you want to keep this here?"

"It's okay here for the time being. I'll eventually figure out a permanent place for it."

Elise sat next to him on the couch. "She is so good."

"Most of the time." Giving her a wry smile, he leaned closer and hoped she wouldn't move away. Thankful that she'd stayed put, he spoke barely above a whisper. "I guess she hasn't erupted into one of her tantrums around you."

Wide-eyed, Elise stared at him. "No. I don't believe it."

"Believe it. That's why they call it the 'terrible twos.'"

"Oh, yeah, my cousin Val has mentioned that."

"Then you know she's not good all the time."

Standing, Elise turned toward the kitchen. "While Olivia is cooking some plastic food for you, I'll make some real food."

Seth reached out and caught hold of Elise's arm. He thought maybe he was dreaming or hadn't heard her correctly. "You're staying longer? You're cooking for me?"

Turning back to look at him, she nodded. "How do you and Olivia expect to eat if I don't fix you something? Besides, I've been doing this every night for Olivia while you've been in the nursing home. I'm used to it."

"I could order a pizza."

"Oh, okay, if that's what you want to do." Elise looked at Olivia, then back at him. "Guess I'll be going then. I just wanted to drop the kitchen off for Olivia."

Seth wanted to kick himself. Elise had brought Olivia a gift, and he hadn't even thanked her. Now she thought he expected her to leave. He didn't mean for her to go. If only he'd thought twice before opening his mouth. He'd wanted to let her know she shouldn't have to fix their meal, that she'd done enough already, but it had come out all wrong. "Wait. I never meant you should leave. Let me treat you, unless you don't like pizza."

"I like pizza, or did you forget? Spinach and mushroom."

He remembered.

He remembered everything—everything about the pizza and everything about the love they used to share. Most of the time remembering hurt because the memories created a longing for her love that he feared he could never realize again. He'd only begun to recognize how much he cared for Elise when the whole incident with Sophie had erupted. He'd had too many casual relationships with women. So when real love found its way into his heart, he hadn't been prepared to deal with it.

Sighing, he shook his head. She had him so discombobulated that he wasn't saying what he intended to say. "I didn't forget. I didn't know whether you'd want to share a pizza with us. Olivia and I would love to have you stay. Will you be our guest? It's the least we can do after all you've done for us."

Seth watched Elise's expression. He could almost see her warring with herself as she contemplated his question. Did he dare enlist Olivia in his cause, or would that be cheating? He was sure Elise would stay for Olivia.

"Will Olivia eat spinach and mushrooms?"

Seth smiled, relief washing over him. "Maybe not, but we can order half cheese and half spinach and mushroom."

"Okay."

"So that means you're staying?"

Nodding, Elise finally smiled. "I never turn down spinach-and-mushroom pizza."

"Great." Seth clomped on his crutches over to the end table next to the brown leather couch and picked up his cell phone. "Can you recommend a good pizza place?"

"Sure. My—"

"Let me guess. Your cousin's pizzeria, right?"

"No. My dad's cousin's wife's brother's pizzeria." Elise laughed, and the sound wound its way into Seth's heart.

Shaking his head, Seth chuckled. "Okay. I'm not going to keep all of that straight. Can you give me the number?"

As he made the call, he leaned against the doorjamb so he could see Olivia busy at work, gathering her pots and pans on the stove and pretending to stir something.

How many make-believe tea parties had he attended in the past year? The older his daughter got, the more her imagination grew. Seth watched his little girl as an ache settled around his heart. He wanted to be the best father he could be, but he wanted more than just the two of them, for his sake and for Olivia's. He wished Elise could be there always to help him, not just tonight. Maybe if he took things slow and easy, she would fall in love with him again.

After he ordered the pizza, he glanced at Elise. "Is all this stuff safe for her?"

Elise nodded. "I only bought the things that said they were safe for two-year-olds. I even took out a couple of pieces that seemed too small."

"That's good." Seth released a long slow breath and wondered whether he'd said the wrong thing again. Did she think he didn't trust her to pick out age-appropriate toys? He was second-guessing himself again.

His brain was as muddled as it had been while he'd been under the influence of the pain medication. He'd never had this much trouble talking with women or asking women for dates. But nothing had been riding on those relationships. Now all his hopes and dreams were wound up in reconciling with Elise, and he seemed to be making a mess of everything he said. Where was the guy who used to be so glib? Maybe when he was around Elise he should be a quiet, more cautious man. Then he might be less apt to say the wrong thing. He hoped the pizza would arrive soon.

While they waited for the pizza, Olivia served Seth and Elise a meal of plastic steak and corn on the cob, which they pretended to eat with great relish. When the doorbell rang, Olivia raced to answer it.

Seth tried to stop her. "Olivia, don't answer the door until Daddy gets there."

"I'll get it." Elise caught Olivia up in her arms and carried her to the front door.

Seth hobbled after them and managed to pay for the pizza. He was really beginning to realize how the crutches limited his movement. How was he going to manage a rambunctious toddler while on them? Getting out of the nursing home made for more problems than he'd anticipated.

Olivia skipped beside Elise as she took the pizza to the kitchen.

Seth stood by, feeling quite useless as Elise set the table. He was certainly glad she'd agreed to stay. How was he going to take care of his house? He supposed he would have to hire someone to clean it. He was giving himself a headache thinking about what lay ahead.

After Elise set the table, she helped Olivia into the booster seat strapped to one of the kitchen chairs. Seth settled on the chair beside her and laid his crutches on the floor.

Olivia held out one hand to Seth. "Pray?"

"Sure." Seth took her hand and then glanced at Elise. "We hold hands when we pray. Something my parents did."

"Okay." Offering a hand to Olivia, Elise gave him a tentative glance before placing her hand in his.

Bowing his head, Seth prepared to pray. He tried not to think of how completely right her hand felt in his. After he finished the prayer, she immediately let go of his hand, but their eyes met before she had a chance to look away. He wasn't quite sure what emotion he'd seen in her eyes—maybe just an awareness that sparked between them.

Seth tried not to think about it as he concentrated on cutting Olivia's pizza into little pieces. Seth and Elise ate quietly while Olivia talked about her new kitchen almost nonstop in her toddler talk that sometimes only he could understand.

At first, when Olivia was doing all the talking, Seth feared Elise and he wouldn't be able to find anything to talk about. He should quit thinking about himself and ask about her life. That had been his problem all along. He was always thinking about himself rather than others.

"You look so serious. What are you thinking about?" Elise squinted at him.

"I've got a lot on my mind, but let's not talk about me. I want to talk about you." That was a good start, but would Elise tell him about her life here in Kellerville?

"Not much to say. School, work and church are pretty much all there is. Not too exciting." She took a bite of pizza, as if to say she didn't want to talk about herself.

"You must do something for fun. Do you still sing?" He'd love to hear her sing again. Her voice was incredible.

"For church."

"No other times?"

"A little karaoke with my dad. He loves karaoke."

"Your dad sings, too?"

Nodding, Elise chuckled. "Juliane and I inherited our singing voices from Dad. Mom's a bit of a monotone."

"I'd like to hear your dad sing."

"You'll get your chance over Memorial Day. Our family always has a big picnic out at Mom and Dad's place after the Memorial Day parade. And whenever we have a family get-together, you can count on my dad revving up the karaoke machine."

"I'd like to hear that."

"It's a fun time." Elise's eyes grew wide, as if she suddenly realized what she'd done—inadvertently invited him to the family picnic. Her alarm dashed his hopes that he was making some headway. He didn't want her to feel bound by the invitation.

"I'm sure it is. I've enjoyed getting to know your dad better over the past couple of weeks when he came to visit me. And Nathan and Lukas, too. I'd hate to miss the fun, but I'll probably be going to Pittsburgh for the holiday, if I'm able to walk without these crutches by then." He pointed to the crutches. "Got to get rid of those things first."

"Well, if you're around, I'm sure my family would love to have you."

Would you love to have me? Seth wanted to ask the question, but he feared what her answer would be. So he smiled and figured she felt safe in telling him to come because he probably wouldn't.

After they finished eating, Olivia ran off to play with her kitchen while Seth tried to help Elise with the cleanup. He made several inept attempts to remove things from the table but found it tricky because of his crutches.

Elise glanced at him with sympathy in her eyes. "You're having a little difficulty, aren't you?"

"Seems that way. I'll get better with practice."

"Since you can't drive, how are you going to get to work?"

"Your dad, Lukas and several of the men from the church have volunteered to take turns chauffeuring me around."

"Dad never said anything to me about it."

"That's because your dad likes to help others without taking credit for himself." Seth leaned against the kitchen counter and looked into her eyes, thankful that she didn't turn away. He wanted to tell her so much, but he wasn't sure whether he could express all that he was feeling, especially about her. He took a deep breath. At least he could let her know how much he'd come to appreciate his fellow Christians. "When it came to Christianity, I was a real skeptic. But I've come to realize over the last year how wonderful it is to be a Christian."

"In what ways?" Elise looked at him with interest, and he smiled as he realized he'd chosen a good topic to hold her attention. Elise had always had strong faith, even if she had drifted from Christian living while on the cruise ship.

"I've seen how Christians help each other." He motioned around the room with one hand. "I'm a stranger in town, and yet people from the church helped me move in here. I saw the same thing when my father died. The members of my mother's church were there to support her."

"I'm glad you're getting the help you need." A little frown puckered Elise's brow.

"Me, too." How many times had he noticed that facial expression on Elise? What was troubling her? Did she believe he was saying these things to get on her good side? He wished he had the nerve to ask, but despite the hours they'd spent together today and all of the nice things she'd done for him, she still held him at arms' length. He wanted to make her smile, not frown. "And you've been a big part of that help. Thanks for all you've done, especially today with Olivia's kitchen."

"You're welcome. I'm glad I could help." She turned away and put the last dish in the dishwasher. "Really. It was nothing. I saw how much my cousin's little girl likes her kitchen, so I thought Olivia should have one. This has been a tough time for her, too. It's hard on little kids when their routine is shattered."

"And thanks for trying to keep a routine for her." Seth released a heavy sigh again. "I hate that you're having to do all the work."

She closed the dishwasher and turned to look at him. "Don't worry about it. I'm here to help."

Seth wished she were here because she wanted to be with him. Hoping to send his thoughts in another direction, Seth looked through the doorway into the living room at Olivia. She was talking on the little toy phone in her kitchen. Wanting to share the scene with Elise, he started to get her attention but changed his mind.

Did being with Olivia make Elise think of Sophie and how he'd turned her away? The question continued to nag him. He couldn't erase the scene with Sophie in Key West from his mind. The guilt ate at him even though he was now taking care of Olivia, especially when he remembered how he'd argued with Elise about it later. God had forgiven him. Why couldn't he forgive himself?

Elise joined him in the doorway. "Look at Olivia talking on her phone. Isn't she sweet?"

"Yeah, I think so. I'm glad you think so, too." Seth's voice sounded husky even to his own ears. Her observation warmed his heart.

"Would you like me to help you get her ready for bed?"

"When have you been putting her to bed?"

"Around seven-thirty." Elise raised her eyebrows. "Is that okay?"

"Sure. I wanted to know what kind of routine she's been on so I can keep it the same."

"Your mom said she usually went to bed about that time."

"Did you have any trouble?" Seth realized he should've been asking these kinds of questions before, but he didn't want Elise to think he didn't trust her to take care of Olivia. Maybe she thought he wasn't a very good father because he hadn't asked.

"No. She's been a little jewel. I was surprised, with all the commotion and changes she's been through. Your mom did a great job keeping her on a schedule, and I tried to do the same."

"I think *you're* the jewel for doing this." Standing so close to Elise in the doorway, Seth had to keep himself from reaching out and pulling her into his arms. He wanted to hold her and taste her tender kisses again. He couldn't let himself think about Elise in those terms. She wasn't ready for that kind of relationship with him. He wondered whether she'd ever be. Shoving away from the doorway, he clomped into the living room.

She followed him. "Don't give me any compliments. Sometime, I might ask you to return the favor."

He wasn't sure what kind of favor she might ask, but whatever it was, he was willing to grant it. He owed her a lot. And he wanted to give her even more. He glanced down at Olivia. "Hey, sweetheart, it's time to get ready for bed."

"No. Play."

Elise hunkered down next to Olivia. "Olivia, honey, you can play tomorrow. We can get your jammies on and read a book like we've been doing, okay? You know how much you like your stories before bed."

"'Kay." Olivia held her arms out to Elise. "Stories, stories. Love stories."

Picking up Olivia, Elise stood, then headed back toward Olivia's room. Elise's ability to persuade Olivia to leave her kitchen filled him with amazement. As they headed to her bedroom, he brought up the rear. In minutes, Elise had Olivia making a game of getting into her pajamas and brushing her teeth. After she was ready for bed, she picked out a book and gave it to Elise.

Elise looked up at him. "Do you want to read her the story tonight?"

"I do."

"I thought so."

After laying his crutches aside, Seth carefully sank onto the padded rocking chair, and Elise handed him the book. Olivia scrambled up to sit on his lap. He opened the book and began to read. Contentment settled in his mind. Everything was perfect—perfect except one thing. He wanted Elise to be a permanent part of this picture, not just a visitor. But he wasn't going to let his thoughts follow that trail. Not tonight.

As soon as he finished the book, Olivia hopped down and ran over to Elise, who was sitting on the edge of the white toddler bed. His mom had told him about taking Olivia to buy the pink coverlet embroidered with butterflies for Olivia's bed. Little puffy pillow-like decorations hung on the wall behind the bed. All the pink spelled Olivia, and she looked adorable surrounded by it, especially when she smiled up at Elise.

"'Lise, say prayers."

Elise nodded. "Okay."

Olivia knelt beside her bed, folded her little hands and bowed her head. Seth stayed in the rocker and bowed his head. Elise began a simple prayer, then Olivia followed with her own version in words that probably only she and the Lord understood, ending with a prayer for Seth to get better. His heart swelled with love for his little girl *and* the woman beside her. He wasn't doing very well when it came to not thinking about Elise in terms of family.

After the prayer, Olivia hopped into bed without protest. Elise leaned down and gave Olivia a good-night kiss. Seth hobbled to the bedside and gave Olivia a kiss, too.

Seth turned on Olivia's butterfly nightlight, then shut off the overhead light in the room. He followed Elise out of the room as quietly as he could while dragging a cast and propelling himself forward with his crutches.

Elise grabbed her purse and slung the strap over her shoulder, then turned. "Got to head home."

Seth didn't know how he could thank her, but he had to say something, even something inadequate. Before he could figure out how to say thank you, Olivia came bounding into the living room. She grabbed hold of one of Elise's legs and held on.

"'Lise, stay with Daddy and me."

Elise stared at him, panic radiating from her eyes. She appeared to swallow a lump in her throat as she dropped her purse and picked up Olivia. "Olivia, sweetie, I can't stay. I was only here because your daddy couldn't come home until he was better. Now he's here, so I need to go to my own house."

Olivia wrapped her arms around Elise's neck and buried her face on Elise's shoulder and cried. "Nooo."

"I'm so sorry I can't stay, but if you go to bed like a good girl, I promise to come visit you as often as I can. And if your daddy needs someone to watch you while he's gone, I'll come anytime, okay?"

While Elise comforted his child, Seth held his breath. He felt as though a huge weight were pressing down on his chest. As he watched them, he realized that Olivia's words had voiced what he'd been thinking, how badly he wished Elise was his wife, and that his home was *theirs* to share.

He wanted Elise to know that, but he knew it was far too soon. Elise wasn't ready to hear that yet, to be told that he loved her—had never stopped loving her.

Olivia lifted her head and looked at Elise. "'Kay."

"Good. Let's take you back to bed." Elise gave his daughter a hug. Without looking his way, Elise nearly fled down the hall to Olivia's room.

When Elise returned, she grabbed her purse from the floor and rushed to the door. "I'm out of here. I want to be gone if she gets out of bed again. Good night."

Shouting his thanks, Seth hobbled to the doorway as she raced to her car. After that initial panicked look, Elise had refused to meet his gaze. She'd looked all around him, but she'd never made eye contact. What had she been thinking?

As Seth watched her drive away, he had no doubt she was running away from him and the memories that hurt them both.

Chapter Eight

"I can't help you plan this party." Elise jammed her fingers through her hair, then held her hands on top of her head as she stared at Juliane. "I can't deal with Seth."

Crossing her arms, Juliane shook her head. "I don't get it. For the last week you've been going over to his house every night to fix his supper. So what's the problem with planning a housewarming party?"

"If I help plan it, I'd probably have to attend it."

"So?"

"So I don't want to socialize with Seth."

Juliane made a choking sound. "Run that by me again."

"No. You heard what I said."

"But it doesn't make sense." Juliane wrinkled her brow. "You see him all the time—at church, at his house and when you go to work out at the rec center."

"I don't see him when I work out. I go over to his house because I pick up Olivia and take her home from day care. I fix their supper, then leave. I leave as soon as he steps in the door. I don't spend time there when Seth is there. I only go because I promised Olivia I would."

"I thought you'd resolved all your issues with him. I thought you were friends." Juliane waved her hand in front of Elise's face. "Elise, talk to me. Tell me what's bothering you."

Elise sank onto the couch and stared at the floor. How could she explain everything to Juliane? Would she even understand?

"I'm waiting." Juliane joined Elise on the couch.

Elise looked up and read the sympathy in her sister's eyes. Maybe she needed to talk to someone rather than carrying this thing around inside. "Okay. Don't judge me."

Juliane gave her a wide-eyed, exasperated look. "Why do you always say that?"

"'Cuz you're the perfect daughter."

Juliane reached over and playfully slapped Elise's arm with both hands. "Stop saying that. No one's perfect but God."

"I know, but you didn't go off and live like a heathen for six years."

Juliane laughed. "But we've got you home safe and sound now. So stop dodging the question. What's the problem with spending time with Seth?"

"I can't be friends with Seth."

"Why not?"

"Because he's a temptation I'm not sure I can resist."

Juliane frowned. "And what does that mean exactly?"

Elise let out a heavy sigh, then launched into a play-by-play of the day she'd taken the toy kitchen to Olivia. As Elise came to the end of the story, her pulse pounded in her brain. "When Olivia asked me to stay, I took one look at Seth and went weak-kneed with panic. I…I wished I could. I wanted to be part of that family, to be a mother to Olivia and…"

"And be Seth's wife? So I guess that answers my question at last. You do still have feelings for him."

"It doesn't make any difference. How could we have a relationship after what happened? How could I trust him after the way he kept secrets from me before? When the secrets were exposed, he made it very clear that I had no business interfering in his choices, that I had no say in what he did. That I didn't matter enough to be a real and lasting part of his life. He didn't love me, Juliane. He didn't love me then, and he doesn't love me now."

"But you still love him?"

"That still wouldn't be a good excuse for falling into a relationship with him again. Besides, I don't love him, not anymore. I've moved on, just as he has."

"I don't think you're admitting to yourself how you feel about him."

Elise laid her head on the back of the couch and stared at the ceiling. "No. That's not it. I'm just confused about the way he makes me feel."

"And how is that?"

"I thought I was getting used to being around him. I didn't mind taking Olivia to visit him. Then the other night happened, and it was like something out of one of those dreams I used to have of the life we'd build together. It took me back to the beginning of our relationship, when I was so sure it would last." Elise sighed again. "I thought we were happy then, but now I'm not even sure about that."

"Maybe you need to figure out your feelings. Be brave and quit hiding from them."

Raising her head, Elise waved a hand at Juliane. "See? You're even the brave one. I'm a wimp. I don't want to think about it."

Juliane cleared her throat. "I'm not that brave, and you're not a wimp. You're forgetting how I wasn't brave enough to share Dad's problem with Lukas, even though he would've been the best person to understand because of his own battle with alcohol. And I was afraid to deal with my feelings for Lukas. So I understand what you're going through."

"But it's not the same."

"Not exactly, but both are about overcoming past hurts. If I could tackle the embarrassment of Dad's alcoholism, then you can tackle your feelings and figure out where your heart is. Do you have any idea how he feels about you?"

"He's just sorry about the way things ended with us." Elise shrugged. "He wants to show me how he's changed his life."

"Then you should let him."

"I don't want to have to deal with him, but it's like I'm stuck."

"What do you mean?"

Elise bit the side of her lower lip. "I've grown to love Olivia. There's no doubt I love that child. When she puts her little arms around my neck, it's the best feeling. I never want to let go."

"Then don't. See where these mixed up feelings for Seth and Olivia take you."

Shaking her head, Elise laughed halfheartedly. "I'm thinking that can't be a good idea. It'll just make me want to bring back a relationship that probably never should have happened in the first place. Aren't we supposed to flee from temptation?" Elise eyed Juliane. "Hanging around with Seth certainly isn't doing that."

"Okay, you make a good point." Juliane slowly nodded. "But I'm going to pray about this, and you should, too."

Elise knew that was something she hadn't been doing. She'd prayed for his recovery, but she'd failed to pray about her feelings for him. "You're right, Jules. Thanks."

"Okay, now that we've settled that, we have to work on the housewarming party."

Elise narrowed her gaze. "You're not going to let this party thing go, are you?"

"No, I'm not. Mom is counting on you to help. What will everyone think if you don't?"

"Maybe I don't care what everyone thinks."

"What will Olivia think if everyone is there but you?"

"You don't play fair, do you?" Elise picked up the decorative pillow lying beside her on the couch and threw it at Juliane.

"No." Juliane threw the pillow back.

Elise caught it and hugged it to herself. "Okay, you win. I'll help plan the party, but I'll have to work on my attitude."

"Well, just think about doing it for Olivia. That should make you feel better about it."

"Yeah, it should." Elise didn't argue the fact that doing this for Olivia still wasn't going to wipe away the fact that this party was also for Seth. Could she be brave? She'd managed to be brave enough to visit him in the hospital. She'd managed to be there for Olivia even though it meant running into Seth every day for a few minutes. So she could be brave enough to help plan this party, go to the party and be friendly to Seth without letting the past trigger unwanted feelings. The first two were completely doable—the last one…doubtful.

Conversation and laughter sounded throughout Seth's house. Church members, people who worked with Seth at the recreation center, Keller family members and friends mingled in the living room and kitchen and spilled into the yard. The sun beamed down from a cloudless sky and warmed the mid-May Saturday afternoon. God had provided a perfect day for the housewarming.

As Elise kept a watchful eye on Seth from the kitchen, she prayed that God would provide her with peace of mind and a way to sort out her feelings concerning Seth. Thankfully, since she'd arrived, other than saying hello, she hadn't had to interact with him. His other guests kept him occupied.

Helping prepare food, Elise looked through the kitchen window at the activity in the backyard. Her cousins Val and

Carrie supervised their children, Olivia and several other children of varying ages as they played either on the wooden swing set or the sandbox at the back of Seth's large corner lot. Lukas and Nathan had organized a coed Wiffle Ball game, and they were choosing teams. Elise watched as one by one the captains chose their teams. When Lukas chose Seth, a loud cheer erupted. Much backslapping and high-fives made the rounds as he greeted the other members of the team.

Elise shook her head. How could he possibly play a game of Wiffle Ball when he was dragging the big cast on his leg and walking with the aid of crutches, even if there was no base running in the game? The lyrics from an old song from her parents' era, "It's My Party," skipped through Elise's mind as she watched Seth. He wasn't going to cry at his party, but he was going to do as he pleased, even if it meant pushing the envelope concerning his recovery. Or was she judging him too quickly? Maybe he was going to occupy the bench as a cheerleader.

Elise's theory about Seth as a cheerleader was soon disproved. When his team took the field, he put on a baseball glove and propelled himself to the triple-play area. Incredible. How was he going to catch a ball if it didn't come right to him?

Shaking her head again, she also wondered how he could possibly bat while he stood on crutches. Here was the same old Seth—doing what suited him no matter the consequences. He kept saying he'd changed, but how much? He was still driven by his impulses, letting them push him into bad decisions. But did his newfound faith help to add God's direction to his choices? She wasn't sure. If she continued to hide out in the kitchen and never interact with him, how was she ever going to make that determination?

While Elise stood there, debating with herself about what she should do, her mother came over and took the bowl of potato salad out of her hand. "You've done enough work today. I see how you're watching the activities with a little yearning in your eyes, so go out there and have some fun. And tell your dad not to overdo. He's not as young as he used to be."

"Mom, Dad's not going to listen to me. You can remind him in the morning when his muscles are sore." Elise laughed, thinking about the one trait that Seth and her father had in common—the tendency not to listen to other people's advice.

Hurrying outside, Elise knew her mother couldn't possibly have known what she was thinking, but God knew. So maybe He had prompted her mother to step in and give Elise a little nudge. She also couldn't ignore her mother's comment about the yearning in her eyes. Had she been yearning? For what? Seth?

How was she going to figure things out if yearnings got in the way? She pushed the question from her mind as she approached Nathan, whose team was at bat. "Hey, Nathan, got room for another player?"

Nathan came over and draped an arm around Elise's shoulders. "Always room for you, Elise. You can play in the triple area of the field, and you'll be the last batter."

"Okay."

While her team was up to bat, Elise settled in one of the lawn chairs that served as the bench. She watched Seth to see what he was going to do if a ball was hit near him. Eric Wilson, Carrie's husband, was the first batter for their team. He popped a ball up to the double-area player, who caught it with no difficulty. Nathan came up to bat next and hit a single to give the team an imaginary runner on first base. The following two batters struck out. That made Elise the first batter in the next inning.

She trotted out toward the triple area. She passed Seth, who was moving quite rapidly on his crutches.

Stopping, he grinned at her. "Good to see you out here. I'm going to hit one over your head for a home run."

"We'll see about that." Grinning back, she halted and gave him a pointed look. "Good thing for you there's no base running in this game."

"A great game for me and my backyard."

"I still think you're crazy to be out here on those crutches."

"I'm getting pretty good on these things." He gave his crutches a pat.

"Don't get too smug."

"Remember my warning." He saluted and continued toward the lawn chairs.

As she took her place in the triple area, she breathed a sigh of relief. Thankfully, while she'd been talking with Seth, she'd had none of those awkward feelings from the night she'd brought Olivia the kitchen. Talking to him had felt comfortable and easy, like their interactions on the ship before their romantic relationship had begun. Maybe dealing with Seth wasn't going to be so bad after all. Maybe she'd been worrying for nothing. Everything was under control.

Juliane was the first batter for Lukas's team, and she popped a ball up to the pitcher. Then Lukas came up to bat. He hit a ball high in the air. It sailed toward Elise. She lifted her glove and caught it. When she threw it back to Nathan, she noticed Seth watching her. He gave her a thumbs-up sign, but his smug little smile told her he was reminding her that she wasn't going to catch the ball he would hit. The next batter struck out, and Seth's team took the field.

This time as she passed Seth, he grinned at her again. "You think you can hit something past me?"

"I'm making no predictions, unlike someone else I know."

"Afraid you can't hit one, is that it?"

"I'll let my bat speak for me."

Seth laughed out loud. "I'll be waiting."

Elise took her stance in the batter's box.

Seth leaned on his crutches and yelled, "Swing, batter, batter, batter."

She tried to ignore Seth's loud chatter, but suddenly his constant attention was making her heart race. Why was she letting him bother her? She swung at the first pitch and missed. Seth continued his obnoxious attempt to distract her.

Elise was determined to quiet him. As Nathan wound up, she put every ounce of her concentration into hitting the ball. She swung the bat, and it connected. Pop! She hit a line drive that went into the double area untouched. Her teammates erupted in cheers. They gave her high-fives as she returned to the bench.

Not daring to glance in Seth's direction, Elise took a seat. She didn't want to look at him. All his teasing was starting to play havoc with her carefully laid plans. She didn't want to let his presence in her life resurrect feelings from the past. As she sat there stewing, she realized she'd made an unreasonable plan. The feelings had already been resurrected. The new plan had to make sense of them—put them in a proper perspective—because trying to bury them again was impossible.

When the game was over, Lukas's team had won thanks to Seth's home run. As he predicted, he hit a ball well over Elise's head. And despite his limited ability to move, he managed to catch a few balls that popped up in his area.

As they gathered near the picnic table piled with food, Nathan clapped Seth on the back. "Congratulations on leading your team to victory. We'll have to have a rematch."

"You're going to give him a big head." Elise frowned at Nathan.

Nathan shook his head. "Not if we come out ahead in the rematch."

"I'm going to be harder to beat next time, because I won't have these crutches."

"Don't be too sure. We had to let you win this time because you're the guest of honor and disabled besides." Elise gave him an impish grin. "What kind of party hosts would we be if we beat the guest of honor?"

Winking, Seth gave her a lazy smile. "Okay, just keep teasing. I can do a little of my own."

"I'm sure you will. You're good at that." A fluttery feeling hit Elise in the pit of her stomach. Was she ever going to get passed these crazy responses? She'd been doing so well today trying to be Seth's friend. She wanted to race into the house so she could get away from him and gain her equilibrium. But before she could make her move, her mother quieted the crowd as she clanged a couple of pot lids together.

"Okay, folks, Pastor Rob is going to give thanks for the food, then our guests of honor, Seth and Olivia, can head up the food line, and everyone else can follow."

Everyone bowed for prayer, and Elise tried to quietly shuffle away from Seth. As Pastor Rob began the prayer, Elise felt a small body clinging to her. She opened her eyes. With her arms wrapped around Elise's leg, Olivia smiled up at her. The little girl's smile melted Elise's heart. Father and daughter were making a mess of Elise's emotions.

The prayer ended, and Elise picked Olivia up. "Have you been playing with all the other kids?"

Nodding, Olivia pointed toward the swing set. "I swinged a lot."

Dismay on her face, Barbara came over to them. "I wasn't thinking. Poor Seth can't get his food while he's on those crutches, and he can't help Olivia." Barbara laid one hand on

Elise's arm. "Dear, will you help Olivia get her food while I help Seth?"

"Sure." Glad for an excuse to leave Seth behind, Elise took hold of Olivia's hand and led her to the end of the table where the plates were stacked.

Elise took Olivia down the table of food and filled her plate with her requests and got food for herself. After settling Olivia at a nearby picnic table, Elise cast a glance at Seth and her mother. She'd taken charge as if he were a five-year-old instead of a grown man of thirty. He appeared to be enjoying the attention as he laughed at something her mother said.

Another thing that hadn't changed.

He'd always liked being the center of attention, but at the same time, he enjoyed meeting and being with people. He was a people person, effortlessly charming and engaging. That's what had made him a wonderful cruise director.

Elise couldn't take her eyes off of Seth. That tiny corner of her heart that he still seemed to possess grew a little larger as she watched him laugh with her mother and grandmother. He charmed women of all ages—like the nurses and little old ladies at the nursing home who had hated to see him leave.

Forcing her attention on something besides Seth, Elise helped Olivia cut her meat into small pieces. "Is that okay?"

Olivia nodded and looked across the table. "Hi, Daddy."

Elise jerked her head up. Grinning at her, Seth stood on the other side of the table as he leaned on his crutches. Her heart zinged like one of the Wiffle Balls that she'd hit during their game. She couldn't get around her attraction to him, but she was determined to keep it contained. She would deal with it somehow.

Her mother set his plate on the table, and her grandmother placed a lawn chair at the end of the table where Olivia sat. "Do you need help sitting in the chair, young man?"

"Thanks, but I can manage now." Gracing the older women with one of his signature smiles, Seth eased himself down onto the chair, then laid his crutches aside.

Elise's grandmother patted Seth on the shoulder. "Now if you need anything, let us know."

"Thanks, but I'll be fine." Seth turned his attention to Olivia. "So how's my girl? Did Elise get you some good food?"

Munching on a carrot, Olivia nodded. "'Lise my friend."

"She's a good friend, isn't she?" Seth fixed his eyes on Elise. They seemed to project unspoken questions. *What about you? Are you my friend, too?*

Olivia nodded again. "She gots me cake."

Seth laughed out loud. "That makes her an especially good friend."

"Was she not supposed to have cake?" Elise's heart sank.

"No, that was my mom's rule, but I still try to limit her sweets, so cake is a treat." Seth laughed again. "I see she's eating carrots, too. That's good."

Elise pretended to wipe perspiration from her brow. "Whew! Glad I'm not in trouble."

"No need to worry. I don't know what I'd have done without you these past few weeks. I haven't thanked you enough." He leaned forward. "You hardly give me a chance to say thanks when you run off as soon as I get home."

"I have to get home to study, so I don't have time to hang around." Elise wondered whether he had any clue why she'd been doing that.

"Oh, okay." He winked. "I was beginning to think you were running off because you didn't like me."

Elise wasn't sure how to take his comment. They'd once been on very intimate terms—something she was struggling not to think about. Was he trying to determine how she felt about him now?

Attempting to put her thoughts in order before she spoke, Elise held her breath as she pressed her lips together. She didn't want to say anything she might regret later. She was beginning to see that she might be falling into the same old trap of liking him too much for her own good. Letting that happen, before she figured out what he truly wanted, would be a big mistake—the kind of mistake she'd made in their previous relationship. He'd changed, but had those changes made him ready for love?

Sometimes she thought he had, but too often she saw the same old Seth, flirtatious and charming and never fully serious. She wanted to be sure before she let down her guard and allowed herself to let him into her life. She was having a hard time holding on to that resolve.

She tried to smile. "In fact, I was going to tell you that I won't be able pick Olivia up after day care or fix supper this coming week. I have to go with Juliane on Monday to get our dresses fitted for the wedding, and the rest of the week I have to study for finals."

"You should've told me you didn't have time. I would've made other arrangements." He lowered his head for a moment. When he met her gaze again, his expression was apologetic. "I've taken your help for granted. I didn't mean to take advantage."

"It's okay. It hasn't been a problem until this coming week. I need all my time for studying." Elise wondered whether he'd taken their past relationship for granted. Had he expected her to fall for him as soon as he indicated his interest? Did he expect that now?

"I understand. I'll see if I can make arrangements to have Olivia stay longer at day care. And your mom and a bunch of other ladies have filled my freezer with meals of every description. I won't go hungry."

"And if you need any help, as my grandmother said, I'm sure Mom can get someone from the Ladies' Circle to come and assist you." Elise placed a hand over her heart. "I wanted you to explain to Olivia why I can't be there."

"Nothing like leaving the difficult job for me." Smiling ruefully, he glanced at Olivia, who was busy eating, then back at Elise. "Are you sure you don't want to do it? You did a great job talking to her the other night."

Elise's mind seemed to freeze as if to keep out any thoughts about that night. Not daring to look at Seth, she took a deep breath to calm herself. She slowly released it as her anxiety faded. "I—"

"Okay. I get it. It's my responsibility. But I think I'll wait till everyone leaves." He grinned. "If I have trouble, can I call you?"

"You won't have trouble." Elise smiled as her own troubling thoughts disappeared. The attraction for Seth was still there, but she had it under control. Or maybe she was finally letting God be in control of her thoughts.

"Mind if we join you?" Carrying a plate loaded with food, Lukas stopped next to Seth.

Juliane stepped up beside Lukas. "We were at the end of the line. Good thing there was a lot of food."

Elise nodded, glad for some company to put some distance between her and Seth. "I'll scoot over here next to Olivia and give you some room to sit."

Juliane took a seat next to Elise. "Can you believe we're actually having a party without having Dad drag out his karaoke machine?"

"He's probably saving his voice for the Memorial Day party." Elise chuckled. "Or maybe your wedding reception."

Juliane groaned. "Absolutely not. I already told Dad there would be no karaoke at the wedding reception."

"How did he take that?"

"Very well, actually." Juliane gazed adoringly at Lukas and looped her arms through his. "I can't believe the wedding's four weeks away."

Elise took in her sister's happiness and tried not to think of Seth in context of weddings, but she wondered whether he would be at Juliane and Lukas's wedding. He probably would, since he and Lukas had become friends. Hopefully her duties as maid of honor would keep her too busy to spend time with Seth.

Seth looked Elise's way. "Since you mentioned the Memorial Day party, I hope I'm still invited. My mom called the other day and said she's coming to visit that weekend. She didn't want to take the chance that she wouldn't see Olivia if I still wasn't able to travel by then. Maybe she's even coming to see whether I've recovered, but I'm used to playing second fiddle to Olivia."

"That's great." Lukas clapped Seth on the back. "Now you'll get to hear Ray Keller and his famous karaoke. At least it's famous here in Kellerville."

Seth didn't take his eyes off of Elise. "And I expect to hear Elise sing, too."

Elise's heart raced at the thought of singing for Seth. She didn't know why. She'd sung in front of him hundreds of times while they'd been working for the cruise line, but everything was different now. She didn't know how to act around him anymore, and events like the Memorial Day party were putting him in her path more than she wanted. She loved his little girl, but she couldn't interpret her feelings for him. How was she going to handle this roller coaster of emotions?

Chapter Nine

Elise rushed into Keller's Variety as her dad was turning out the lights at the front of the store. "Are Val and Carrie here?"

"Well, hello to you, too." Ray chuckled as he pulled the shades on the front doors.

"Hi, Dad." She gave him a peck on the cheek. "Didn't mean to ignore you, but I've been in a rush. Had my first final."

"How'd that go?"

"I think I did pretty well."

"Great. And to answer your question, no, Val and Carrie aren't here. Neither is your mother. She called and said she and your aunt Charlotte are running late, but your sister's in the back, unpacking the dresses."

"Good. Aren't you going to stick around to help?"

Chuckling, Ray knitted his shaggy eyebrows. "What would I do except get in the way? I'm not hanging around for this hen party. Besides, isn't it bad luck or something to see the wedding dress ahead of time?"

"I think that's supposed to apply to the groom, not the father of the bride."

"Oh, I see. Guess I'd better get this wedding thing down.

I'm thinking it looks like I might be footing the bill for another one soon." Ray gave her a speculative glance.

Her stomach sinking, Elise shook her head. "I don't know where you're getting that idea."

"Observation."

Elise wasn't sure she wanted to know what her dad was observing, but her curiosity won out. "What observations?"

"You and Seth."

"Dad, I don't know what you think you're seeing, but you've got it all wrong."

Ray nodded his head. "Okay. I'll take your word for it." He waved a hand at her. "I'm out of here. I'm going to let you girls handle it."

"Okay, Dad. See you later." Elise watched him go, glad that he wasn't interested in pursuing any discussion about Seth. But she had a feeling he really didn't believe her when she'd told him he was wrong.

Hoping to erase any thought of Seth from her mind, Elise hurried to the back of the store, where she found Juliane. "Did all the dresses come in?"

Juliane looked up from the group of boxes she was inspecting. "Yes, and I'm getting ready to unpack them."

"Let's do your dress first." Elise stepped closer. "Is your dress in this box?"

Juliane nodded. "Help me get it out."

Elise held the flaps of the box back as Juliane took out the packing material and unfolded the wedding dress. Elise ran her hand over the white beaded chiffon. "Juliane, the dress is beautiful. In the months since you ordered it, I've forgotten how pretty it is."

Juliane put it on a hanger and held it up. "It's even better than I remembered. Help me get into it before Aunt Charlotte gets here to measure for the alterations."

"Sure." Elise watched Juliane disappear into the dressing

room. "Do you want me to open the other boxes while you're getting ready to put the dress on?"

"Okay, but listen for Val and Carrie. They said they'd be here as soon as their husbands got home to babysit."

"I will." Elise opened the remaining boxes and took out the slate-blue chiffon-and-satin bridesmaid dresses. She carefully hung them up on a nearby rack. "Did Dad tell you Mom and Aunt Charlotte are going to be late?"

"Yeah. I'm ready to put the dress on." Juliane's muffled voice sounded from inside the fitting room.

Elise brought the strapless gown in and held it while Juliane stepped into it. After Elise zipped it up, Juliane stood on the round platform in front of the triple mirror. Elise had never seen her sister so beautiful. "Juliane, the dress is so right for you. You'll bowl Lukas over when he sees you in it. I like it even better than when you first tried it on."

"Me, too."

"And it almost fits you perfectly without any alterations."

Glancing down, Juliane lifted the skirt. "It has to be shortened."

"I've got your shoes right here." Elise opened the bag sitting next to her on the floor and pulled out a pair of strappy white sandals. "I love these shoes, too."

Juliane took the shoes. "While I'm getting fitted, you need to try on your dress. Carrie and Val should be here any minute to try theirs on, too."

"Speaking of Val and Carrie, we were talking the other day at church, and we decided we're going to take you to Newport on the Levee for a bachelorette party."

"No bachelorette party."

"Yes." Elise narrowed her gaze as she stared at Juliane. "We have it all planned."

"Aren't bridal showers enough?"

"No. Besides, Nathan is having a bachelor party for Lukas.

The guys are all going to a Reds game. So you need a bachelorette party, as well."

Juliane sighed. "Okay. So what are your plans?"

"We'll go to the aquarium, then out to lunch. Whatever you'd like."

"You know my input. Forget the bachelorette party."

"Not possible. We're going to have a girls' fun day even if we have to drag you along. We'll have a great time. Just the four of us, like we used to do."

Juliane laughed. "Sure. I'll have tons of fun while I'm bound and gagged."

"What's the fuss? You're always talking about a trip to the aquarium. So now here's your chance."

Juliane nodded. "Okay. You've convinced me, as long as I get to spend as much time at the aquarium as I want."

"We promise to give you all the time you need."

"So is Seth going to Lukas's bachelor party?"

Elise shrugged. "How would I know? I figured you know more about that than I would."

"You two seemed really chummy at the housewarming, even after all your protests about going to the party."

"That's because of Olivia."

"Did you ever think your interest in Olivia is giving you an excuse to be with Seth?"

Elise didn't say anything for a moment as the question rolled through her mind. Could that be true? She thought about what her dad had said earlier. Was she sending out signals that she didn't even realize? When it came to Seth, she was about as mixed up as she could be. "All I know right now is that I adore his little girl. Could we not talk about him?"

Juliane scrunched her face up in a way that told Elise her request was going to be denied. "We won't talk about him for the rest of the evening if you let me mention one thing, okay?"

Sighing, Elise let her shoulders sag. "Okay. Get it over with."

"Pastor Tom asked Lukas and me if we'd head up the float committee for the Fourth of July parade. We've already got the youth groups and their sponsors helping to make the float."

Elise rolled her eyes toward the ceiling. "So what are you asking me to do?"

"Of course, we're going to do the red, white and blue color scheme with balloons and the stuff we buy every year. In fact, we have some left over from last year—"

"Juliane, I don't need a blow-by-blow of all your plans." Elise put her hands on her hips. "Just get on with what you're expecting me to do."

"Okay, Lukas and I thought it would be fun to have a mixed quartet singing patriotic songs on the float."

"So you want me to sing on the float?"

"Yeah. That's it."

Elise shrugged. "I can do that."

"Good. Then it'll be you, me, Lukas and Seth."

"So this is how Seth comes into the picture? Have you asked him?"

"Well, no, but I'm sure he'll do it."

"Aren't you presuming a lot? Maybe he won't agree to do it, or he's busy doing something else."

"Actually, I wanted to make sure you approved before I asked him." Juliane bit her lower lip.

"What would you do if I say I won't sing with Seth?"

Juliane shrugged. "Get someone else—maybe Stephanie Merkel. I think she kind of has her eye on Seth."

Elise was wise to Juliane's game. She was trying to make Elise jealous. Well, unfortunately, it was working. She didn't want Seth to sing with someone else, especially if that someone had a romantic interest in him. Elise knew her thinking was nuts. She didn't want someone else to have an interest in him until she figured how what was going on in her heart and head when it came to Seth Finley. "I said I'd do it. I just wondered what happens if Seth doesn't agree."

"I'll get down on my knees and beg Nathan to sing." Juliane folded her hands in front of her face, then looked intently at Elise. "You know he's so wrapped up in bank work these days that it seems as though he doesn't have time for anything else."

"You're right. He never comes with us to the coffee shop anymore, but at least he came to Seth's housewarming. And he said he was coming to the Memorial Day party. He has to have his Wiffle Ball rematch."

Before Elise could comment, her mother and her aunt Charlotte came in through the back door. After a hurried greeting, they immediately started fitting Juliane's dress. Moments later, Val and Carrie joined them. Soon the women were laughing, talking and sharing in Juliane's happiness.

Despite her joy for Juliane, Elise's heart had that tiny pinprick of jealousy. Would she ever find love like Juliane had? Was Seth meant to be part of that picture? Is that why he'd shown up in Elise's life again?

The sun flitted in and out of the clouds as Seth turned his shiny new silver extended-cab pickup into the driveway leading to Ray and Barbara Keller's house. Seth found a spot to park in the grass off to one side among the cars that lined both sides of the driveway. After so many weeks of being unable to drive, he felt like a kid with his first car. But a chill had run down his spine when he'd driven by the spot where his car had skidded off the road. Would that happen every time he drove out here to the Kellers' house?

As he switched off the ignition, he glanced over at his mother, then at Olivia in the backseat. "We're here. Are you ready for a picnic?"

"'Lise here?" Olivia squirmed to get out of her car seat.

"Yes, she'll be here." Seth unbuckled Olivia and hoped his mother wouldn't ask about Elise, especially while Olivia was around. Other than a passing hello at church, he hadn't had any contact with Elise in the past two weeks. Every nerve was on edge at the thought of seeing her again.

Seth helped Olivia out of the car. As soon as her feet hit the ground, she ran ahead.

"Olivia, please wait for Grandma." Maggie hurried ahead to catch her granddaughter.

Olivia turned around and giggled. "Gramma, run."

Maggie chuckled as she chased after her grandchild. "You are keeping me young."

Seth watched them as his mother waylaid Olivia, his heart swelling with love for them. The only thing that would make life better right now was having Elise as part of this family. How was he going to make that happen? Maybe today could be a step in that direction.

He had his life back, or at least most of it. The crutches were history, though he still had to use a cane for support and to keep his balance on rough terrain. The leg that he'd broken was still mending, but it was definitely stronger. There was a bit of a limp in his step, but it was getting less noticeable with each passing day.

Now that he was driving again, and his mother was here to watch Olivia, this would be a good time to ask Elise for a date. In the past, he wouldn't have thought twice about asking a woman out. He'd been confident that any woman would jump at the chance to go out with him. Those days were history.

Losing Elise had changed his perspective. She'd brought his ego down to size. His brash behavior had cost him the only woman he'd ever truly loved. He wasn't sure how to win her back, but he figured taking things slowly would work better than trying to charge back into her life and declare his love.

But he hadn't been counting on the accident to delay things. Was this the right time to ask her out? He didn't have the self-assurance that she would accept if he did. He kept remembering that night when Olivia had asked her to stay and how Elise had practically sprinted out of his house at the first opportunity. What had her running away from him?

This was the time and place where he was supposed to leave the whole thing in God's hands.

As the backyard, filled with picnic tables, lawn chairs and a crowd of people, came into view, Olivia let go of Maggie's hand and raced ahead to where Elise stood, talking with Juliane. Olivia reached up and tugged one of Elise's pant legs. Glancing down, Elise smiled and picked Olivia up.

Seth swallowed a lump in his throat as he observed them together. Today was the day. He prayed that God would give him the opportunity to talk to Elise.

Maggie turned back to Seth with a shrug. "I can't keep up with your daughter. She seems to have a mind of her own—very much like her daddy."

Seth smiled at his mother's assessment. "You're just now noticing this?"

"Well, it's more evident since you've moved away, and I don't see her every day." Maggie took hold of Seth's arm and pulled him to a stop. "Olivia seems to have bonded with Elise."

Seth nodded, wondering where this conversation was headed. "She has."

"And how does that make you feel?"

Leave it to his mom to ask a probing question—one he wasn't sure he could answer. "Most of the time I'm okay with it, except when I have to explain to her why Elise has to go home instead of staying like she did while I was in the nursing home."

"Oh, that is a bit of a problem." Maggie chuckled.

Seth rubbed his chin. "Yeah, tell me about it."

"So how are things between you and Elise?"

"At a standstill."

"And that means…?"

"It means nothing has changed since I moved here."

"You haven't told her how you feel?"

Seth shook his head. "I'm waiting."

"For what?"

"The right time. I don't want to scare her away." Seth sighed. He wasn't about to tell his mother that he intended to have a conversation with Elise today. Right now, that was between him and God.

"I don't think you'll scare her away. She seemed quite concerned about you while you were in the hospital after the accident."

His mother's statement gave him hope, but he didn't want to be too hopeful and find he'd been too optimistic. "That's the kind of person Elise is—the kind who cares for other people. That's why Olivia was drawn to Elise from the very beginning. She cares about my little girl."

Maggie touched his arm. "And I think she still cares about you, too."

"We'll see." He wished he had his mother's conviction, and he hoped she wasn't going to interfere by trying to push Elise and him together. He wanted to do this in his own time and his own way. Then he cautioned himself. Better make that God's time and God's way.

As Seth and Maggie continued toward the gathering in the Kellers' backyard, Elise approached them. She still held Olivia in her arms.

"Hi, Daddy. I finded 'Lise."

"You did." Smiling, Seth glanced at Elise. "Hi. Thanks for including my mother."

Elise looked past him. "Hello, Mrs. Finley. It's good to see you again. I'm so glad you could join us today."

"Thanks. And please call me Maggie."

Elise gave her a tentative smile. "Okay. I'll try to remember."

Maggie surveyed the crowd. "I wanted to say hi to your mother, but I don't see her."

With her free hand, Elise pointed toward the house. "She's in the kitchen, preparing for the big picnic."

"Does she need help?"

Elise shook her head. "She's in there surrounded by most of my aunts, who are helping her. My mom and aunts have these holiday gatherings down to a fine science. If there's any reason to celebrate, the Kellers throw some kind of party. They've got things so well organized that sometimes I think the food serves itself. But I'm sure she'd love for you to stop in and say hello."

"I think I'll do that." Maggie smiled. "I can't tell you how much I appreciated your parents' hospitality when Seth was in the hospital."

"I know my mom enjoyed having you and Olivia at the house. She loves entertaining company."

"Okay, then, I'm headed up there." Maggie gave Olivia a kiss on the cheek. "You keep an eye on your daddy and make sure he uses his cane."

"Daddy and I be good." Pointing toward the group of children playing in the giant sand box at the edge of the yard, Olivia squirmed to get down. "I go play?"

"Okay. Go have fun." Elise set Olivia on the ground, and she toddled off to join the other youngsters.

Seth turned his attention to Elise. "I've graduated. No more crutches."

"I see." Elise smiled. "That's great. How does the leg feel?"

"Good. Doc says I'm making excellent progress." He grinned. "I'm ready for the Wiffle Ball game. Has Nathan got it set up?"

Elise nodded. "He's planning on the game, but since we have more room here than at your place, he intends to play softball rules so more people can play."

"I'm there."

Elise narrowed her gaze. "Your daughter told your mom you'd be good. I'm not sure running bases with or without a cane is being good."

Seth laughed. "Are you concerned that I'll hurt myself?"

"Seth, be serious. You don't want to fall and break your other leg or an arm, do you?"

Seth placed a hand over his heart and gave Elise a deadpan look. "I'm serious. I want to play Wiffle Ball."

Raising her eyebrows, Elise shook her head. "You're not serious. Otherwise, you wouldn't be teasing me and ignoring my advice."

"Does this mean you care about me?"

Elise stared at him as if she weren't sure what to say. "Sure. I care about you. I don't want anything bad to happen to you. You have a little girl to care for."

"I know. Olivia's the most important thing in my life. She's my top priority, so I'm going over to the picnic table near the sandbox, so I can keep an eye on her. Would you like to join me?" Seth wasn't sure what to make of Elise's answer. Did she only care about him because of Olivia, or was there something more personal there?

Elise hesitated as that same wary expression he'd seen before crossed her face. "Okay."

"Great!"

Seth limped alongside Elise as they walked to the picnic table in silence. He could already feel his confidence about asking her out slipping away. He didn't want to be the guy who was too full of himself, but he didn't want to be so diffident that he couldn't get up the nerve to ask Elise for a date.

When they reached the picnic table, Seth vowed to quit thinking about what he wanted. This conversation was the first step in a journey to reconnect with this woman, and he needed to think about her and her wishes.

He waved at Olivia as he sat on the bench, facing outward so he could watch her. "I'm right over here if you need me."

She waved back with her little plastic shovel. "I digged a hole."

"Good job." Seth waved again before he turned his attention to Elise. "Does this gathering include people from both sides of your family?"

"Yes, and friends and neighbors, too. I think this is the biggest party of the year for my dad." Elise glanced over to where her dad was talking with a group of men while they readied the big built-in barbeque grill to cook the meat.

"Is your dad in charge of the grilling?"

Elise nodded. "And the singing."

"Yeah. I'm waiting to hear your dad sing, and you, too."

"Have I told you that you have the most adorable daughter?" Elise's brandy-colored eyes showed genuine affection for Olivia as she changed the topic of conversation. Seth went with the flow, not wanting to push.

"No, but your actions have told me. I think she's adorable myself, but I'm prejudiced. I guess you figured that out." Seth knew his past actions had told Elise that he was a very self-centered man. He wanted to show her with every fiber of his being that he was a different man now. He was capable of prioritizing other people over himself—especially if the people included his daughter, or Elise.

"Yeah, I can pretty much tell she's got you wrapped around her little finger." Elise laughed.

"I have to confess. That's probably true." Seth leaned back

against the picnic table and hoped to get her to talk about herself. "How did your finals go?"

"Good."

"So are you done and have the summer off?"

"No. I'm taking classes during the summer session, but I get my degree in August."

"That's super! Then what are you going to do? Any job prospects?"

Shaking her head, she grimaced. "Not a huge demand for music teachers these days—special ed, yes, but that's definitely not my calling."

"No openings for music teachers in Kellerville?"

"I was hoping one of them would retire at the end of the year, but they all plan to stay at least one more year. Mom told me that today after she talked to one of my aunts who works in the district office." Elise shrugged. "I guess I'm going to have to send out applications to school districts in other places."

"So you'd move away from Kellerville?" Seth didn't want to believe it. Wouldn't that be a cruel joke, if she moved just months after he'd taken a job here?

"Not what I want, but looks like I'll have to."

Seth's heart sank. How was he supposed to win her back if she moved away? Maybe this was the answer from God that Seth didn't want to hear.

No. He wasn't ready to give up. He wasn't going to take no for an answer. Not yet. Somehow things would work out, or God would make it completely clear that Elise wasn't supposed to be part of his life.

Seth wanted to take her hand in his and comfort her and tell her everything would work out for the best. But he gripped the edges of the bench to keep his hands to himself. She might not welcome his comfort, but he could at least tell her he didn't want her to go. "I hope something works out so you don't have to move."

"Thanks." Elise smiled. "Me, too."

Her smile made Seth's heart race. He should quit wasting time and ask her out. She'd agreed to sit with him here. That had to be a good sign.

As he was about to open his mouth, Juliane rushed up to them, her breath coming in gulps. "Lukas's grandfather drove his car into the ditch about a mile up the road."

Elise jumped up from the bench. "Is Ferd okay?"

Juliane nodded and pointed toward the house. "He's right over there. I think he's a little shaken, but he's fine."

After grabbing his cane, Seth stood. "If he drove his car into the ditch, how did he get here?"

"He walked, and Dot, too." Juliane looked back toward the house. "Lukas and some of the other men drove over there, thinking they could push the car out, but we've had so much rain lately that they can't push it out. It's really stuck in the mud."

Seth took a step forward. "Is there anything I can do to help?"

"Yes, that's why Lukas called on me. He said he thought you had a tow strap in your pickup truck. Do you?"

"I do."

"Good. They want to use it to pull Ferd's car out of the ditch." Juliane flipped open her cell phone. "I'll call Lukas and let him know."

"Tell him I'm on my way." Seth turned back to Elise. "Will you watch Olivia for me?"

"Of course." Elise reached out and grabbed his arm, pulling him to a stop. "Be careful and let the other guys do the pushing, okay? I don't want anything else to happen to you, especially now that you're getting better."

His pulse pounding, he grinned. "I'm sure they're going to want me to drive my pickup, not push the car."

As he limped away, he couldn't help thinking about the lost

opportunity to ask Elise for a date. Maybe he'd lost this chance, but her reaction told him that she cared more than a little bit about him. That gave him hope. The day wasn't over.

Chapter Ten

"Looks like someone has recaptured your heart."

Hearing Juliane's voice, Elise whirled around and glared at her sister. "What's that supposed to mean?"

"You tell me. You seemed awfully concerned about Seth."

"Can't I care what happens to him without you jumping to all kinds of wild conclusions?"

"Are they wild?"

"Yes." Elise didn't even want to discuss it, but she knew Juliane wouldn't let it go. "I know how he is, and he'd go headlong into helping when he shouldn't. He has to think about Olivia."

"Oh, so that's how it is, huh?"

Elise held up her hands. "Okay, you don't have to tell me. I should mind my own business, but he did ask me to keep an eye on her. And…"

Juliane gave Elise a hug. "It's okay. But I think you should be honest with yourself and examine your feelings about Seth."

Elise sighed. "You keep telling me that. I have, and I haven't figured out one thing. I'm still as confused as ever."

"Well, at least that's a start."

"How?"

"You're admitting your confused feelings to me instead of ignoring the subject." Juliane grinned.

Elise laughed halfheartedly. "Yeah. And don't go sharing that with anyone."

"You can count on me." Juliane did the locking-lips routine again.

Elise laughed out loud. "I love having you for a sister."

"That's not what you said when we were in high school."

"Yeah, I know, but isn't it great to grow up and find out we can be friends?"

"It is."

Elise glanced at the sandbox. "I'd better do my duty here and keep an eye on Olivia."

"And I'm going up to the house to help serve the food." Juliane started to walk away, then turned back. "Save a spot for Lukas and me, so we can all eat together, okay?"

"I will." Elise resumed her spot at the picnic table and watched Olivia as she played with the other kids.

As the minutes ticked by, Elise enjoyed observing the little girl's interaction with her playmates. Even at two and a half, Olivia already had her father's ability to charm her companions. She'd already stolen Elise's heart. Was that what was drawing her to Seth, too? Was she admitting Juliane was right—that Seth had recaptured her heart? No. He still had a long way to go in that regard, but he was definitely softening her resolve to keep her distance. She wasn't sure what she wanted to do about it. Let it happen, or resist?

"We got the car out of the ditch, and I'm still in one piece." Seth's voice sounded behind her.

Her heart racing, Elise took a calming breath before she turned to find Seth standing on the other side of the table. "That's good. Did you find out why he went into the ditch?"

Seth nodded. "Just like me, he swerved to avoid hitting a

deer. That's a dangerous stretch of road. At least his car only went into the ditch."

"Did this bring back the memories of your accident?"

"It did."

"I'm so sorry." Elise couldn't imagine reliving the horrific event.

Seth rubbed the back of his neck. "You know, I want to remember the best thing about that day—your dad praying with me and telling me to hang on while they got me out of that car."

A lump rose in Elise's throat. Turning to look at Olivia in the sandbox so Seth couldn't see, she blinked rapidly to suppress the tears stinging her eyes. Seth had lived through the terrible accident, but it hurt Elise to think of what might have happened without her father's help. With her emotions finally under control, she faced him. "I'm glad he did. And now that you're back, I'm going up to the house to help with the last-minute food prep. See you later." She started to sprint toward the house.

"Elise."

She stopped. "What?"

"I hope you're planning to eat with Olivia and me."

"And Juliane and Lukas." She raced away before he could say anything else. She wasn't ready to face what was happening. Now that Seth didn't need her help to get through his recovery, spending time with him had a whole new dimension. She had to decide how their relationship would move forward.

After Elise got her food, she found a seat at the picnic table where she and Seth had sat earlier. Lukas and Juliane soon joined Elise, putting their plates on the table across from her.

"Hey, how's my sister-in-law-to-be?" Lukas stood by as Juliane scooted across the bench.

"Good." That was, if she ignored her nervous anticipation about Seth sitting nearby. At least Juliane and Lukas would serve as a buffer.

"I understand Juliane has talked you into joining us on the church float during the Fourth of July parade." Lukas took a bite of his hamburger.

"She has." Elise wondered what this would entail. She'd been afraid to ask.

Laying down her fork, Juliane looked at Elise. "Speaking of that, do you think you and Seth could get together to go over some songs?"

Elise narrowed her gaze. "I can't speak for Seth. Have you talked to him about it?"

Juliane nodded. "I mentioned it to him at church, and he agreed to do it."

"That's good." Elise wondered why Seth hadn't mentioned it while they were watching Olivia.

"I'm glad to hear you say so." Juliane took a sip of her lemonade.

A puzzled frown knitting his brow, Lukas looked from Juliane to Elise. "Am I missing something here?"

Elise bit her lower lip as she glanced up at Lukas. Obviously, Juliane hadn't shared with Lukas any information about Elise's relationship with Seth. Elise was grateful for Juliane's silence, but Lukas might as well know what was going on. Elise let out a heavy sigh. "Yeah, here's the deal. Seth and I used to be involved when we were working together. It didn't end well. So sometimes things are awkward between us."

Lukas raised his eyebrows. "That explains it. I didn't mean to put you on the spot."

Elise laughed halfheartedly. "That's okay. You didn't know."

Lukas turned and looked at Juliane. "Yeah, how come I didn't know?"

"You know why you didn't know. That was sister stuff I couldn't share." Juliane playfully punched him in the arm.

Lukas held up his arms, pretending to defend himself. "Okay, okay. I won't interfere in the sister stuff. I think that's something I should put in my permanent how-to-be-a-good-husband memory bank."

Elise laughed. "Juliane, I think you're marrying a very smart man."

"Of course, she is." Lukas put an arm around Juliane's shoulders and pulled her close.

Elise took in their good-natured kidding and wished she could be as fortunate as her sister. As Elise continued to eat, she wondered what had become of Seth. She scanned the crowd but didn't see him or Olivia. He was the one who'd asked to sit with her, but he hadn't shown up. Had her response about sitting with Juliane and Lukas made Seth think she wasn't all that interested in eating with him? Why was every decision about Seth accompanied with self-doubt or recriminations?

"How are you guys going to fit all this singing stuff into your schedule with your wedding coming up in two weeks and then your honeymoon?"

"We have two whole weeks before the parade to practice after we get back."

As Elise took a big bite of her hamburger, she saw Seth maneuvering his way through the picnic tables. Maggie walked close behind him as she helped Olivia with her plate. Olivia appeared unnaturally subdued. Where had they been all this time?

"Looks like you guys are almost done eating. Were you thinking we weren't coming?" Seth set his plate on the table, then picked up Olivia and helped her onto the bench at Elise's end.

Elise wondered whether she wanted to admit she'd been

thinking about him. *Quit being silly. Be a grown-up.* "I did wonder what had happened to you."

"We had a little problem." Seth glanced at his daughter. "Olivia spilled her first plate of food down the front of her clothes. We had to change them, then get more food."

"Thankfully, before we left home, I convinced Seth he needed to bring an extra set of clothes for Olivia." Maggie put Olivia's plate in front of her, then sat at the end of the bench on the other side of her granddaughter.

Seth laid his cane against the picnic table and sat in between Olivia and Elise.

"Me sit by 'Lise." Olivia looked at Seth with her little face all scrunched up.

Seth eyed Elise. "Seems you're very popular today."

His scrutiny made Elise's heart race. "What would you like me to do?"

"I'll sit on the end, and you can sit next to Olivia." Seth smiled. "Guess I'm playing second fiddle to you."

"She gets to see you all of the time."

"Is that it?" Seth got up and waited for Elise to scoot down the bench.

Elise glanced over at Seth as he sat on the end of the bench. "I'm just guessing."

"I miss 'Lise."

"I miss you, too." Elise leaned over and put an arm around Olivia's shoulder and gave her a squeeze.

As Elise straightened, Seth was staring at her. She didn't know what to say. Even if she did know, she wouldn't be able to say it because of the lump in her throat. His little girl was tugging on her heartstrings. How could this child be expected to understand why Elise had been her caregiver for two weeks, then had almost dropped out of her life completely? No wonder Olivia was clingy. She should make it up to Olivia somehow, and that somehow would probably involve Seth.

While they ate, Elise wondered how she was going to handle singing with Seth and being a part of his daughter's life without letting go of her heart. How was she going to know what God wanted rather than what she wanted?

After everyone had finished eating, Nathan gathered the group who wanted to play Wiffle Ball. He tried to keep the original teams for a rematch of the game played at Seth's housewarming party, and the captains chose new players to add to those original teams.

Elise joined the group as she eyed Seth, who had left Olivia in Maggie's care. How was he going to play ball? Silly question. If he could play while on crutches, he could play while using a cane. She'd already warned him against playing, but he'd just teased her.

Nathan explained the rules and the boundaries. Again Elise and Seth were on opposite teams. He grinned at her as he limped to first base.

Elise's team had two hits but scored no runs in the first inning. Surprisingly, Seth did a fine job at first base. She got ready to take her position in the outfield.

As she passed Seth, he winked. "Be prepared to chase the ball, because I'm going to put one over your head again."

Elise laughed. "I'm prepared. You were true to your word in the last game."

The score seesawed back and forth. As they came to the last inning, both teams had scored six runs. Seth had failed to get on base. He'd hit a fly ball that had been caught in the outfield each time he'd been up to bat.

When Elise's team took the field in the top of the last inning, she stopped as she passed by Seth. "I'm still waiting for you to hit one over my head. This is your last chance."

He gave her a smug look. "I've been saving the best for last. Be prepared."

Shaking her head, she smiled. "Don't get too cocky."

"I've heard that before."

Elise took her place in left field. When Seth came up to bat, his team had runner on first base. As he took his place in the batter's box, he looked out at left field. He was looking right at her. Would he really be able to hit one over her head?

Seth swung at the first pitch and fouled it down the third-base line. Elise retrieved it. When she threw it back to the pitcher, Seth pointed in her direction. "I'm aiming your way."

Elise cupped her hands around her mouth. "You'd better improve your aim."

As Seth got ready for the next pitch, a little voice sounded from the group of spectators sitting in lawn chairs. "Daddy, hit the ball."

Seth waved at Olivia. "Okay, sweetheart. I'm going to hit one just for you."

With the next swing of his bat, Seth sent one right over Elise's head and across the boundary line for a home run. His teammates cheered as he rounded the bases with his gimpy stride. When he reached third base, Olivia bounded onto the field to greet him. Seth stopped and picked her up and carried her to home plate. Elise couldn't even muster any disappointment that her team was losing. Her heart melted as Olivia hugged Seth's neck. He set her on the ground, and she scampered away to rejoin Maggie on the sidelines.

Elise wanted to hug Seth's neck, too. She pushed that thought away as she got ready for the next batter. That kind of thinking could only get her into trouble. Seth's homer had put his team ahead by two runs.

When Elise's team came off the field, she stopped by first base where Seth stood. "Congratulations on your home run, but the game's not over yet."

He gave her a lopsided grin. "So you think your team can make a come back and beat us?"

Elise nodded. "The heart of our lineup is coming up."

"We'll see." Seth pounded his fist into his glove.

Elise trotted away, trying not to think about the way Seth was worming his way into her heart again. Little by little he was showing her that he was a different man than the one he'd been, yet he'd kept all the charm and playfulness that she'd loved in him from the first.

Elise's team didn't score while they were at bat, so Seth's team won. The losers gathered the bats, balls and bases. While laughter and good-natured ribbing floated through the group, everyone shook hands all around.

Seth came over to Elise and extended his hand. "Good game."

Elise quickly shook his hand, trying not to let his touch do crazy things to her insides. She forced herself to think about the game and not about how Seth was making her feel. "Did Nathan say anything about a rematch?"

Seth laughed. "No, but seems as though you think there should be one. I didn't know you were so competitive."

"There are a lot of things you don't know about me."

"I know, and I want to change that." A serious look crossed his face. "Since I got rid of my crutches, Olivia and I are going to celebrate. My mom told me your mom invited her to go out to dinner with some of the ladies from church on Thursday night, so Olivia and I will be on our own. We've decided to go to the Dairy Barn to eat. Will you come with us?"

Unsure of her answer, Elise looked at him. The question went right to the heart of everything she'd been thinking over the past few weeks—the past few hours. Was she willing to let Seth back into her life? Was she strong enough to handle it if she fell for him again and he still wasn't ready to love her? But did it really matter, when she might be moving anyway?

Elise let courage wash away her fear for at least today. "Sure. I'd like to celebrate with Olivia and you. And you did okay playing Wiffle Ball today, too. I guess I shouldn't have been worried."

He smiled wryly. "I'm glad you cared enough to worry."

Elise looked away, realizing how much she was beginning to care. The thought pricked her heart with a little doubt. But she was determined to face her fears and work through them.

With his gimpy gait, Seth fell into step beside Elise as she strolled toward the house. "Are you ready for karaoke? Looks like your dad has it all set up."

Stopping, Elise put a hand on one hip as she gaze at Seth. "Are you sure *you're* ready? You've never—"

"What do you mean I've never done karaoke? On the cruise ship I was in charge of karaoke hundreds of times."

Elise laughed. "If you'd let me finish, I was going to say you've never been involved with one of my dad's karaoke sessions. He always manages to get people involved even when they don't intend to sing. It's the peer pressure or something. Uncle Carl is the only person my dad is still after to sing."

"Maybe I can get your uncle to sing. What do you think?"

"I'm not sure you want to hear him sing." Elise chuckled. "He really can't carry a tune."

"That's the beauty of karaoke. You don't have to be able to sing." Seth glanced around the yard, then back at Elise. "I want you to introduce me to your uncle Carl, so I can convince him to sing."

Laughing, Elise shook her head. "You'll never get my uncle to sing. Never."

"If you introduce me to him, I'll have him singing before your dad puts away the karaoke machine today."

Elise took in Seth's statement. Here he was again confidently predicting what would happen, as he'd done during the Wiffle Ball game. He'd done the same thing when he'd boldly predicted she'd fall for him when he'd first approached her on the cruise ship.

The memory made her want to look away, so she occupied herself with looking around for her uncle. Elise spotted him talking with a group of men under the shade of the red maple trees bordering the property. She turned to Seth and nodded in her uncle's direction. "He's the tall balding man in the blue shirt."

Seth grinned. "If I get your uncle to sing, I think I should get some kind of reward. What do you think?"

"And what kind of reward are you thinking you should get?"

Seth wrinkled his brow as if he were thinking hard. "So many choices." Then he winked. "I've got it. You have to sing one song I choose and sing another one with me. My choice also."

"What if I don't agree that you should have a reward?"

Seth shrugged. "Guess you won't get to hear your uncle sing."

"I'm not the one who wants to hear my uncle sing. I said my dad's been trying to get him to sing."

Seth turned toward the house where Ray was making the final check on the karaoke system. "Then I'll go talk to your dad."

As Seth limped away, Elise wondered what kind of bargain her dad would make with Seth. It could be worse. She remembered her dad's comment about another wedding in his future, and she knew he wouldn't hesitate to do a little matchmaking. Maybe it would be better to have this whole reward thing under her own control rather than letting Seth negotiate with her dad.

Elise hurried after Seth. "Seth, wait."

Turning, he grinned. "Change your mind?"

She tried not to let her agitation show. "Yes. If you get my uncle to sing, I'll do what you asked. But you have to get him to sing."

"Great." His grin widened. "Let's go over there now, so you can introduce me."

Elise walked with Seth across the yard. She made the introductions, then excused herself, leaving Seth on his own to deal with Uncle Carl. From a distance, she watched them talking. Seth said something, and Uncle Carl laughed. As they continued to talk, she wished she'd stayed so she could hear what they were saying.

While Elise stewed about what was being discussed in the huddled group of men, her dad got up on the deck and used the microphone to get everyone's attention. Most of the crowd began moving toward the deck, bringing lawn chairs and picnic benches with them. Elise grabbed a lawn chair and looked for Juliane and Lukas. Spying them, she headed their way.

Ray began to sing one of his favorite songs, "Impossible Dream." As Elise listened to her dad's wonderful tenor voice, she placed her chair next to Juliane's. A few seconds later, Seth put his chair down next to hers.

When Ray was finished and the applause died down, Elise turned to Seth. "Where's Olivia?"

"She's playing in the sandbox again. My mom's watching her."

"Did you convince Uncle Carl to sing?"

"You'll have to wait and see."

Seth leaned toward Elise. "Your dad has a great voice. No wonder he likes to do karaoke. So how does this work?"

"Dad has a list of songs that are available. They're up on the deck if you want one. And he has his little bowl of names. He draws them out, and people sing." Elise chuckled. "Now that he's updated his collection, even some of the teenagers sing because he actually has something they know."

Juliane leaned across Elise. "That's not entirely true. The teens can sing the oldies, too. They've listened to enough of them over the years."

Standing, Lukas reached across Juliane and Elise as he waved a piece of paper. "Here's the song list, if you want it."

Seth reached out and took it. "Thanks."

Elise watched Seth as he perused the list. "So you must not have convinced my uncle to sing."

"What makes you say that?" He looked at her with a grin.

Elise pointed to the song list. "You haven't even looked at the song list."

"Now I have, and I know which song I'm going to have you sing. It's the one I enjoyed hearing you sing the most."

"Which one?"

"You'll find out after Carl sings."

Seth got up and walked over to Uncle Carl, who sat at a picnic table near the edge of the yard. While Seth talked with Carl, Elise tried to guess which song Seth was talking about. He'd never told her he had a favorite.

As Seth returned to his seat, Elise tried to read his expression. But his demeanor gave her no clue as to what had transpired during his conversation with Carl. "All set?"

"Like I said, you'll have to wait and see."

While a steady stream of singers paraded across the deck, apprehension grew in Elise's mind. She wished she knew what to expect. Would she have to sing with Seth, or was he stringing her along, making her think he'd convinced Carl to sing?

Finally, Seth and Nathan got up on the deck and sang "Whenever God Shines His Light." Next they sang "Bless the Broken Road," a song made popular by Rascal Flatts.

Seth seemed to be singing right to her. Was her own broken road leading back to Seth?

Before Elise had time to contemplate the question, she saw Uncle Carl heading for the deck. She couldn't believe what she was seeing. How had Seth talked her uncle into singing?

"Hey, everyone, we've got a real treat for you." Seth shook hands with Carl as he hopped up on the deck. "Carl here is going to lead you in a sing-along. So let's give a big round of applause for him, and everyone join in the song."

As applause filled the backyard, Elise glanced over at Juliane, who looked as stunned as Elise felt. Carl took the microphone and soon had the whole crowd singing "Sweet Caroline" at the top of their voices.

More applause followed after they finished, and Seth gave her a look that told her she was now going to have to sing. Elise saw no point in delaying. After Carl left the deck, she went directly up there and stood next to Seth. Her heart pounding, she waited for his instructions.

He smiled—not a smile of triumph, but one telling her he was glad to have her by his side. He brought the song up on the screen. "Okay, folks, Elise and I are going to sing a duet, 'You've Got a Friend.'"

Elise started the song tentatively, but as she sang she forgot about any problems with Seth. Their voices blended and she lost herself in the song. Singing was what she loved.

When they finished, the crowd applauded and cheered. Elise wondered whether Seth meant to send her a message with his choice of songs. Was he just looking for friendship and forgiveness while she was worrying about something much more? Maybe she was fretting for nothing and setting herself up for more heartache.

After showing her the song he'd chosen for her solo, Seth stepped to one side of the deck. "Now Elise is going to sing a song that she sang hundreds of times while we worked together on a cruise ship. It's one of my favorites. 'At Last.'"

Taking the microphone, Elise decided she needed to quit trying to read anything into Seth's song choices. He'd just wanted to hear her sing—nothing more. As she sang she realized he was using his charisma on the crowd and on her as he'd done dozens of times when they'd worked together. She was taking one more little step toward letting him back into her life. Was she ready to go along for the ride and see what would happen?

Chapter Eleven

Elise paced back and forth in the living room. She kept telling herself not to be nervous. This was only a trip to the Dairy Barn for one of their delicious cheeseburgers and an ice cream cone. It wasn't really a date. Olivia would be with them.

But Elise couldn't deny that this was a baby step toward the idea of a renewed relationship with Seth. So far she'd worked to maintain distance and to keep her burgeoning feelings for him in check. Were these feelings remnants of the old relationship, or were they something new? What effect would tonight's outing have on her emotions?

Despite her decision to see what might happen with Seth, she had to keep her thoughts under control.

Juliane stepped into the living room. "Will you please sit down? You're driving me nuts."

"I can't sit still."

"Okay. Wear yourself out."

Elise peered out the window, then continued pacing. "You're not one to talk. I remember you doing a little pacing of your own when you had to deal with Lukas after he moved to town."

"No pacing for me. That's what you do. I'll admit I had my

share of anxiety over Lukas, but now that I'm on the other side of all of that anxiety, I see how I worried and stewed for nothing. God will work it out one way or another. So go and enjoy yourself. Have a good time and forget about anything except tonight."

Elise stopped and gazed at her sister. "Easier said than done."

"I know." Juliane hugged Elise.

The doorbell sounded.

"He's here. Do I look okay?" Pulling out the legs of her tan Capri pants, Elise took a deep breath and let it out slowly.

"You look great. Have a good time. I'll make myself scarce." Juliane headed back to her room as Elise went to answer the door.

When she opened the door, Olivia stood there with a bouquet of lilacs in her hand. She shoved them at Elise. "For you 'Lise."

"Thank you, Olivia. These are very nice." Elise took the flowers.

"You're welcomed." Olivia danced into the living room.

Elise buried her nose in the fluffy blooms. "Mmm. They smell wonderful." Elise looked up at Seth. "How'd you know I liked lilacs?"

"Because every day when you left the house while you were coming to fix us dinner, you'd stop and smell the blooms on the bush next to my back door. There aren't many flowers left, but we managed to get a few."

"I appreciate your thoughtfulness." Elise's heart tripped at the thought of Seth taking note of her love of lilacs. "Let me put these in a vase, and then we'll go."

"Me help." Olivia trailed after Elise.

Still holding the flowers in one hand, Elise turned and with her free hand grabbed hold of one of Olivia's hands. "Okay. We can do this together."

Seth's cane thumped against the floor as he followed them to the kitchen. While Elise and Olivia searched in the walk-in pantry for a vase, Seth leaned against the framework of the door going between the living room and the kitchen. He watched them through the open door of the pantry.

Elise was very aware of his scrutiny. Little tingles of excitement rifled through her mind. Her reaction to Seth's presence was exactly what she'd been worried about. She tried to remember Juliane's words about letting God work it all out. God had a plan for her life. She needed to get out of the way and not worry about it.

Elise spied a white vase on the top of the pantry. She handed the flowers to Olivia and reached up to retrieve it. Despite standing on her tiptoes to take advantage of her nearly six-foot height, the vase was inches out of her reach. She poked her head out of the pantry and looked at Seth. "We need your help."

"Sure." He pushed himself away from the doorjamb. "What do you want me to do?"

Elise's pulse jumped as he stood there looking at her. Thoughts of flower vases faded, and the only answer that came to mind at the moment was "kiss me." She clamped her mouth shut, fearful that somehow the words would escape through her lips. She stepped back and pointed. "I can't reach that vase."

"I can get it." Seth stepped farther into the pantry.

His nearness in the close confines made her pulse beat wildly. She took a deep calming breath. Nothing changed. Her heart still racing, she pressed her back against the wall to put distance between them and give him more room to get the vase.

Being a few inches taller than Elise, he reached up with little effort, grabbed the vase and brought it down. Turning, he handed it to her. "Here you go."

"Thanks." Elise took the vase, being careful not to make contact with Seth in any manner. She feared touching him would put her racing heart into overdrive. She wanted to get out of the pantry in the worst way, but he was blocking her exit. She would have to wait until he moved. Trying to take her mind off Seth, she glanced down at Olivia. "Would you like to put the flowers in the vase and carry them to the table?"

Olivia nodded, and Elise held the vase out to the little girl. She fumbled to put the stems of the lilacs into the vase.

Reaching down, Seth assisted her. "Good job."

"Me carry." Olivia lifted her little arms.

Seth glanced at Elise for approval. Elise nodded as she carefully placed the vase in Olivia's little hands.

"Okay. Hold it tight." Seth leaned over and guided her out of the pantry.

Watching, Elise swallowed hard. The chemistry between Seth and her was still there, at least on her side of the equation. She couldn't deny it or ignore it.

Her emotions continued to be so mixed up. Could she ever straighten them out? Was spending time with Seth going to help or make matters worse? Hopefully, their time together tonight would answer some of her questions. Then maybe the attraction wouldn't jump out and assail her.

Elise also had to figure out how much of her fascination with Seth was wrapped up in her feelings for Olivia. The little girl touched Elise's heart in a way she'd never felt before. She'd never cared about another child in this way.

With Seth's help, Olivia put the vase on the kitchen table. She turned and smiled at Elise. "Good?"

"Yes, very good." Elise leaned over and hugged the little girl. "Now let's put some water in the vase."

Elise filled a pitcher with water, then poured it into the vase. She centered it on the table and carefully arranged the flowers so the purple blooms formed a beautiful cluster, then turned to Olivia. "What do you think?"

"Bootiful."

"Yes, they are." Elise picked up Olivia and looked over at Seth. "Thank you again for bringing me the flowers."

"You're very welcome." Seth stepped toward the door. "Ready to go?"

"I'm ready for a great cheeseburger. I can taste it now." Still carrying Olivia, Elise followed Seth out to his pickup and prayed that God would help her find the answers. Where did Seth fit into her life?

The Dairy Barn, an old abandoned barn that had been converted into a restaurant, sat just off the main drag near the edge of town. As Seth pulled into the parking lot, cars snaked around the building as they waited in line for the drive-up window. He found a parking spot, and as he escorted Elise and Olivia into the popular restaurant, he prayed that this evening would go well. The flowers had been a hit, so at least he'd gotten off to a good start.

Families and groups of teenagers, occupying the red faux leather booths, filled the air with laughter and conversation. The young hostess took them to a booth near the front. She gave Olivia a coloring sheet and four basic crayons, then fetched a booster seat for her.

When Olivia insisted on sitting next to Elise, Seth smiled and shook his head as he took a menu from the holder sitting against the wall. "Looks like I'm going to play second fiddle to you again tonight."

Elise glanced over at Olivia who was busy coloring, then looked back at Seth. "I don't think you ever play second fiddle where she's concerned. You're a hero in her eyes."

"Thanks for saying so. I hope that's true." Seth wished he

was a hero in Elise's eyes, as well, but he'd done some unheroic things that he knew she hadn't forgotten, even if he had been forgiven. He was working hard to erase those images, but was Elise seeing the changes?

"It's true. I see the way you love her."

"My world definitely revolves around her." A far cry from the way he'd acted a year and a half ago, in Key West. He didn't even want to think about the man he was back then. God had changed his life and made him a different person.

The waitress appeared and took their order and reappeared a minute later to deliver their drinks.

Olivia tugged on Elise's arm. "See my picher?"

"It's lovely."

"For you, 'Lise." Olivia handed her the paper.

"Thank you. I'll add it to the collection on my refrigerator."

Fiddling with the straw wrapper, Seth tried to calm the anxiety that wouldn't go away. His wish to make this night the beginning of a new relationship with Elise had his nerves on end. "Should I call you 'Lise, too?"

Elise gave Olivia a little hug. "Umm…what do you think, Olivia? Should your daddy call me 'Lise?"

Olivia nodded. "That your name."

"I guess she's given you her permission." Elise chuckled.

Still trying to relax, Seth smiled wryly. "I wasn't asking for her permission. I was asking for yours."

"Oh. I didn't know you ever asked for permission."

Seth wondered what she meant by that statement. Did she still see him as the guy who did what he pleased no matter the consequences or who he hurt? He didn't seem to be making much progress in changing her opinion of him. Should he even comment on it? He'd probably be better off if he ignored it. But he reminded himself that she'd agreed to come to dinner with him. That spelled progress, didn't it? "I knew sooner or later I'd slip up and call you by that name, since Olivia calls you that all the time. She talks about you constantly. 'Lise this and 'Lise that. She's always cooking something for you in her little kitchen."

"Is that a problem?"

"No, I like having you in her life." He wanted to say *he* liked having Elise in *his* life, too, but he cautioned himself to take things slowly. She wasn't ready to hear that from him. This time he wanted to do things right. He'd rushed their physical relationship before—something he regretted deeply now that he was a Christian. He wouldn't make the same mistakes this time.

The food arrived and rescued him from further explanations and troubling thoughts. He grabbed the ketchup and squirted it on his burger and fries. He looked up at Elise. "Want some?"

She shook her head. "Should we pray?"

Seth's stomach sank. He'd forgotten a very important thing. "Sure."

Olivia folded her little hands. "Me pray."

"Okay." Seth hoped Olivia could rescue him.

"God, tanks for the food. Amen."

Elise patted Olivia on the head. "Thank you. That was a very nice prayer."

"You're welcomed." Olivia took a big bite of her grilled cheese sandwich.

"How's the grilled cheese?" Elise popped a fry into her mouth.

"Good." Nodding, Olivia took another bite.

"I didn't think you were a pickup kind of guy."

Elise's comment startled Seth from his thoughts. "What are you talking about?"

"Your new pickup. I was surprised you replaced your car with a truck."

Seth looked out the window. The sun, hovering just above the tree line, glinted off the shiny chrome trim on his vehicle. "I got a great deal on it, and I figured it would be good for hauling stuff for the rec center. It came in handy the other day when Lukas's grandpa drove his car into the ditch. And somehow it seems safer. I can't help thinking about that since I had the accident."

"I guess that makes sense."

"When do your start classes again?" Seth hoped to change the subject. He hated thinking about that accident.

"Next week."

"Any job prospects?" Seth wished somehow he could find a way to keep her in Kellerville.

She shook her head. "I haven't heard of any. The past couple of days I spent a lot of time filling out applications, and I'm not finished yet. Some of those things are like major tests."

Seth chuckled. "That bad?"

"Yes. I can't believe all the questions I have to answer on some of them."

"Where are you applying?"

"School districts in Cincinnati and the surrounding suburbs." Elise shrugged. "To be honest, I'm not very hopeful."

"Why not?"

"Being an August graduate, for one. Being a music teacher, for another."

"Can you do something besides teach?"

"Yeah, but I want to teach. No matter what kind of job I pursue, if it's not teaching here in Kellerville, I'll have to move to the city. Not too many jobs here for music majors. Maybe I should've gone into another field."

"But you love music, and you should use your talent." Seth wished he could give her some encouraging advice. He wanted her to find a job, but he wanted her to stay in Kellerville. How could he make that happen? He wasn't sure the summer was enough time to win her heart. "I'll pray about it."

Elise smiled, but Seth didn't miss the hint of surprise in her eyes. "Thanks. I appreciate that. Sometimes it's hard to remember to rely on God when I want to do it all myself."

"I know what you mean." He was having that exact trouble in his quest to find his way back into her life. He should step back and let God be in charge.

Elise looked at him again as if she were seeing him for the first time. "Do you ever wonder how to know what God wants for your life?"

Touched that she'd look for his insight into a question of faith, he considered his answer carefully. "I really do. Every time I make a decision—even taking the job here."

"I think God will use us wherever we are, even when we don't make the best decision."

"What makes you say that?"

"Maybe I should say it this way. God can take anything and make good out of it."

"Daddy, I done. Now ice cream, please?" Olivia squirmed in her seat as her pronouncement brought an end to Seth and Elise's adult conversation.

"Sweets?" Elise gave Seth an impish grin.

"Remember, we're celebrating."

Olivia bounced on the bench, and her dark curls bounced, too. "No crutches for Daddy."

"That's right. That's what we're celebrating." Catching Elise's attention, Seth hoped they could find a way to finish their talk. "Afterward, could you stay awhile at my place so we can continue our discussion?"

Elise didn't answer right away, and Seth saw her refusal coming as he observed her expression. Was she still uncomfortable being alone with him?

Grimacing, she slowly shook her head. "I'd better not. I

have more applications to fill out. Tomorrow we're meeting with Juliane and Lukas to pick out songs, and that'll eat
up more of my time. Maybe later, after I get all that stuff
done."

"Okay. Sure. I understand. You're really busy right now
and have a lot on your mind."

Despite the fact that Seth was trying to sound sympathetic,
her "maybe" rang loud and clear in his mind. Would there
come a time when she'd be willing to spend time with him
and not have a cast of characters surrounding them? He should
be patient, remembering God's timing and God's will. Sometimes, he had to admit he didn't want to. He wanted his own
time and his own way.

"Thanks for understanding." Elise glanced down at Olivia.
"Ready for that ice cream?"

"Yes."

With perfect timing, the waitress reappeared and took their
dessert order. While they waited for their ice cream, Elise
played a nursery rhyme game with Olivia, who giggled with
delight.

While they ate their ice cream, they talked about the upcoming meeting with Juliane and Lukas and their wedding.
Seth had grown close to Lukas after the accident and was
pleased that Lukas and Juliane had invited him to the wedding. Now he had to find the right time to ask Elise if he could
be her escort. He wanted to do it face-to-face when they were
alone. Would that time ever come?

The next evening, Seth finished reading Olivia a bedtime
story. He closed the book and gave her a kiss, tucking the
covers around her. "Good night, sweetheart."

"Read more, please, Daddy?"

Seth shook his head. "I can't tonight. I have to meet
'Lise."

She sat up. "I go, too."

Realizing his mistake in mentioning Elise, Seth kissed Olivia on the forehead and tucked her back into bed. "Not tonight. We'll see her at church on Sunday."

"'Morrow?"

"No, on Sunday." How was he going to get away without Olivia having a tantrum? Looking over at his mother, who stood in the doorway, Seth tried to convey his helpless feeling.

Maggie caught his dilemma and stepped toward the bed. "You go ahead, Seth. I'll take care of Olivia."

"Thanks, Mom." Seth stood and gave his mother a quick hug, then looked down at his daughter. "You be good for Grandma.

"If you go to sleep now, I'll tell 'Lise what a good girl you've been."

"'Kay." Olivia snuggled down in the covers as Maggie waved him away.

Grabbing his cane, Seth hurried out of the room as fast as the cane would allow. He feared if he lingered Olivia wouldn't stay in bed. He'd been anticipating the meeting with Elise all day. Tonight was another chance to interact with her. He hoped each time they were together would bring them closer.

As he got into his pickup, he thought of how often Olivia talked about Elise. When he'd decided to pursue Elise, he'd had no idea that his little girl would become so fond of her. Olivia's attachment was one more reason why he wanted to rekindle his romance with Elise. Only this time he knew how to treat her better.

When Seth parked his pickup in front of the coffee shop, he could see Elise, Juliane and Lukas sitting at a table near the door. He sat in his pickup and watched Elise for a moment.

Talking and laughing, she appeared relaxed. Would that change when he entered the picture?

So often when they were together, she seemed to be having fun. Then suddenly he'd see that wary look in her eyes. Was she thinking of something from the past, or was she having second thoughts about her association with him in the present? He wanted to make her happy—happy to be with him.

Entering the coffee shop, Seth slowed his step as he tried to calm his racing pulse. He needed to find a little bit of the old Seth. The guy who hadn't been afraid to tell her when they'd first met that she was going to fall for him. But he had to temper that guy, and maybe he'd find the right combination of old and new.

"Hi, everyone." Smiling at Elise, Seth pulled out a chair and sat down, laying his cane aside. "Sorry I'm a little late. I had to read Olivia her bedtime story."

"No problem. Being a dad comes first." Lukas shoved a piece of paper across the table to Seth. "We were working on a list of possible songs. What do you think?"

While Seth perused the list, the waitress came to take his order. He joked with her as he ordered his coffee. After she left, he caught Elise staring at him. She averted her eyes, as if embarrassed to be caught looking his way.

Seth wondered what Elise was thinking, but he pushed away conjecture so he could deal with the business at hand. "How many songs are we going to sing?"

"I'm thinking about four. We can repeat them all along the parade route." Lukas picked up a pen and turned to Juliane. "Each one of us can choose a song."

"That sounds good." Leaning closer to Lukas, Juliane looked at his paper. "Is that the one you want?"

Taking a gulp of his coffee, Seth glanced at Elise. Why was she being so quiet? She'd been talking and laughing before he arrived. Was his presence making her uncomfortable?

Seth smiled, hoping to draw her out of her shell. "Elise, what do you think?"

"Are we singing a cappella? Are we singing harmony in four parts or no parts?" Elise glanced around the table.

"Good questions." Lukas scribbled on his paper. "What does everyone think?"

"With you guys being gone on your honeymoon, are we going to have time to practice harmony?" Seth asked.

"I say we give it a try. If we think it's going to involve more practice than we have time for, then we can sing without parts, okay?"

Glad to see Elise voicing her opinion, Seth nodded. "I agree."

Elise's questions started a spirited discussion, and they spent the next half hour picking out the songs and ironing out the details of getting a good sound system for the float.

After they'd paid the bill, Lukas leaned back in his chair. "Looks like we've got everything settled."

"We do. That's a relief." Juliane let out harsh breath.

"The relief will be getting through your wedding." Looking at Juliane, Elise crumpled her napkin.

Seth wrinkled his brow. "Aren't the bride and groom supposed to be the ones worried about the wedding? The bride, anyway."

Elise waved a hand in the air. "I'm the maid of honor, and I've got all these responsibilities. I'm way more nervous than Juliane."

"The only thing I'm nervous about is what you've got planned for this bachelorette thing on Saturday." Juliane poked Elise's arm.

Elise held up one hand. "Scout's honor. We have nothing planned but a trip to the aquarium and dinner."

Juliane narrowed her gaze. "I'm holding you to that. No practical jokes or embarrassing singing telegrams."

"We might have a gag gift or two. Can you live with that?" Elise asked.

"I suppose." Juliane looked at Seth. "Do you know what Nathan has planned for the bachelor party besides the Reds game?"

"It's a guys' night out, but I don't know whether any gag gifts, singing telegrams or practical jokes are involved." Seth laughed.

"Whatever it is, I can handle it." Lukas put an arm around Juliane's shoulders and pulled her close. "Just enjoy your party, Jules."

Seth glanced from Lukas to Juliane. "Other than Juliane's worry about the bachelorette party, you two are the calmest bride and groom I've ever known."

"That's 'cuz I'm doing all the worrying for them." Elise chuckled.

"I think you're right." Juliane scooted her chair back and stood. "We've got everything settled for the parade float, so we should call it a night."

Seth got up and followed the group to the door, but he didn't want his evening with Elise to end. He wanted to spend more time with her. He wanted to spend time *alone* with her. Would she let him drive her home? After they left the coffee shop, Lukas and Juliane walked arm-in-arm toward his car. Elise followed behind them.

Seth thumped along with his cane as he tried to catch up to her. "Elise."

She turned, a little frown knitting her eyebrows. "Did you want something?"

"Um…yeah. Could I give you a ride home?"

She glanced over at Lukas and Juliane. "I came with them. I don't need a ride home."

"Sure you do." Juliane gave Elise a little shove in his direction. "Lukas and I can always use a little time alone."

Seth grinned. "Yeah. Let the lovebirds have some time to themselves."

Wide-eyed, Elise stared at him. Seth could almost see the thoughts spinning in her head. His heart did a little dance as he waited for her answer.

Chapter Twelve

Elise swallowed a lump in her throat as she realized what accepting Seth's invitation meant. She would be alone with him—really alone. Yet Juliane's statement made it impossible for Elise to turn down his request without blatantly rejecting him. "Okay."

"Great!" Seth turned to Juliane and Lukas. "See you guys later. Enjoy your alone time."

"You, too." Juliane chuckled as she joined Lukas in his car.

If Elise hadn't known better, she might have guessed Juliane had set this whole scenario up ahead of time. She did know better, of course. Juliane was too focused on her wedding to think about setting Elise up with Seth. But obviously, when the opportunity presented itself, Juliane had no trouble pushing Elise into going with him.

Seth punched the button on the remote for the pickup. As the interior light came on, Seth opened her door.

"Thanks." Settling on the leather seat, she took a deep breath. She would deal with this somehow.

"You're welcome." Seth closed the door.

In the seconds before Seth joined her, Elise prayed that

God would give her wisdom in this situation. She wanted to do the right thing as far as Seth was concerned, but she was drowning in a sea of emotions. God was her life preserver.

Gripping the steering wheel, Seth gazed at her. His attention made her heart thud. He looked as though he were about to say something, but instead, he started the engine and backed out of the parking space. He drove to the corner and turned at the town square.

When he stopped at the stop sign, he looked her way again. "Do you have to go home right away, or would you consider taking a drive with me?"

Elise met his gaze. Her heart had been beating fast before, but now it raced in double time. She felt as though it might beat right out of her chest. Taking a deep breath, she broke eye contact as he pulled away from the stop sign. "Where to?"

With his pickup barely moving, he continued around the square. "I thought we could drive out to the lake and take in the sunset."

"I don't know. I still have applications to work on."

"They'll still be there tomorrow."

"And I still won't have a job tomorrow. Besides, are you sure we can get into the park at this time of night?"

"Yeah. I checked." He pointed to the clock on the dashboard. "It's only eight-thirty. They're open till eleven, and the sun sets in about half an hour."

Elise took in that bit of information. So he'd planned for this. It wasn't a spur-of-the moment thought. Maybe this was the right time to find out where they stood with each other. They'd been skirting the issue of their past relationship for weeks. Was she brave enough to find out where things with Seth were headed?

"Okay, but as soon as the sun sets, we have to head back."

"Deal." Smiling, he turned in the direction of the highway that led to the lake.

While he drove, he didn't say anything. He punched the button to turn on the radio, and classical guitar music filled the cab. His choice of music surprised her.

He gave her a sideways glance as they sped down the highway. "You remember the guitar guy who used to play on the cruise from time to time?"

"Is that one of his CDs?"

"Yeah. Great music."

After that snippet of conversation, Seth remained quiet, and Elise wondered what he was thinking. Should she bring up the reason for this little outing? Maybe he intended to continue their conversation from the previous night. Maybe there was no specific reason. Maybe he wanted to spend time with her, so they could get to know each other again. But where was that going to lead? Too many unanswered questions dominated her thoughts.

The ride was his idea, so she should let him take the lead. But before the night was over, she hoped to get the answers to some of those questions.

After a fifteen-minute drive, they arrived at one of the picnic areas near the lake. They got out of the car and traversed the parking lot to the spot where the picnic tables were located. The soft ground near the picnic tables muffled the sound of Seth's cane, which had been so evident on the blacktop. When he reached the table, he laid his cane on it and sat on top of the table, using the bench for a footrest.

Sitting beside him, Elise wondered what to say. Crickets chirped, and a mosquito buzzed by her ear. She swatted at it. "I hope there aren't too many mosquitoes out here tonight."

"I've got some bug spray in the pickup. I'll go get it." Seth hopped up from the table and grabbed his cane.

"You're prepared for everything, aren't you?"

"Not everything." He hobbled away.

Was he talking about their relationship? As he made his way back to the picnic table, Elise watched him, her heart doing a little tap dance. Despite his limp, he was still a striking man—the kind who made women stop and take a second look. But character was so much more important than looks.

When they'd first met, she'd been thrilled to be noticed by the handsome guy that the other women were chasing. At first, their relationship had been nothing more than friendship, with a heavy dose of flirtation. They hadn't become romantically involved for years.

After they finally had, she'd been so worried about holding on to his attention that she'd compromised her morals, a decision she still regretted. She'd invested too much in their relationship, given too much without being sure of his feelings for her. It was a mistake she wouldn't make again. Were things different now? She was beginning to think so. His frame of reference had changed. A newfound faith in God was making Seth a better man. She wanted to know what that could mean for their future relationship.

After they applied the bug spray, Elise remained standing. She looked out across the lake to where the sun was disappearing behind the line of trees that looked black against the red-and-orange sky. The colors reflected in the lake made the scene twice as beautiful. She glanced over at Seth. "Thanks for convincing me to come watch the sunset with you. It's gorgeous."

"I agree. Nathan told me I wouldn't be sorry if I came out here to see a sunset. And I'm glad you're here to share it with me." He patted the table. "Sit beside me."

In the dusky light, Elise studied his handsome face. She had the urge to throw her arms around him. Stepping away, she closed her eyes.

"Elise, is something wrong?"

"I'm not sure how to act around you." There. She'd finally told him how she felt. Letting her eyes flutter open, she waited for his response.

With the sunset reflected in his dark eyes, he stared back at her. He opened his mouth as he started to say something, but then closed it again. Getting up, still not saying a word, he grabbed his cane from the table and approached her. He stopped a foot away. "We need to talk about it."

"What are we going to say? What can erase the past?"

Seth shook his head. "We can't erase the past. We can't ignore the fact that we shared a relationship. All we can do is try to start over…if that's what you want."

Afraid of her response to him, Elise turned away. Even though she didn't know what the right decision was, she wanted to fall into his embrace. Her heart hammering, she longed to feel his strong arms around her. She took a step back. "But we can't let ourselves rush into anything this time."

"I promise I won't let that happen, if you're willing to give me another shot."

"What are you saying?"

"I'm saying I still care about you very much." His Adam's apple bobbed. "I want a second chance."

The fact that he was nervous and had opened himself up for rejection touched her, but she still had doubts about him. "I'm not sure how I feel about you."

"I understand that, but I think you still have some feelings for me."

Elise laughed halfheartedly. "Yeah, confusing ones."

"Well, that's a start anyway." Leaning on his cane, he grinned. "Is there any possibility I can talk you into letting me be your escort for Lukas and Juliane's wedding?"

"Are you asking me for a date?"

"I am."

Elise let the implications run through her mind. He wanted

a second chance, and she was beginning to believe he deserved one. They both needed a second chance. "Let me think about it, okay? I promise I'll have an answer for you soon."

Disappointment flickered in his eyes, but he still smiled. "Sure."

"I'm warning you, even if I say yes, I'm going to be busy doing the maid-of-honor stuff."

"That's okay. I promise if you say yes, you won't regret it. I'm going to do everything in my power to make up for the wrong I did in the past." He held out his hand. "Let's go back to town. We can talk on the way."

Elise stared at his outstretched hand. Did she dare put her hand in his? Yes. She had to take the chance. Stepping nearer, she slipped her hand into his. His strong fingers closed around her hand as they walked toward his pickup. Contentment settled around her heart. Fear and worry still remained, but she could ignore them for now. With God's help, she was going to face the future and find out if Seth was a man she could truly love.

The following Saturday morning, Elise ushered Juliane toward the entrance of the Newport Aquarium. Elise pointed upward. "Look at this gorgeous day—blue skies and bright sunshine. What more could you ask for?"

"A little more sleep."

"Quit complaining, Juliane. Val, Carrie and I have a fun day planned."

"You call getting up at seven in the morning fun? You promised not to make my life miserable with this bachelorette thing." Juliane frowned.

Elise laughed. "And as I recall, I only promised there would be no practical jokes or singing telegrams."

"Why the early start when the place isn't even open yet?" Juliane waved a hand toward the entrance.

"I told you before—we didn't want to miss the penguin parade."

"And I said we could miss it."

Elise placed her hands on her hips, then glanced at Val and Carrie. "What are we going to do with the grumpy bride-to-be?"

"Got me." Shrugging, Val laughed.

Carrie joined in the laughter. "If we can't have practical jokes or singing telegrams, we had to have something to make you uncomfortable. What would a bachelorette party be without it?"

"That's why I didn't want a bachelorette party." Juliane glared at Elise. "I'll remember this when it's your turn. And I see that turn coming real soon."

"Your imagination is working overtime."

Shaking her head, Juliane grinned. "I wasn't imagining the way Seth looked at you the other night when he asked to drive you home. He's not hiding his interest."

"He was just going along with your request to be alone with Lukas."

"Yeah. I'm sure that's the only reason he drove you home." Juliane raised her eyebrows. "That's why a five-minute trip took over an hour. What did you talk about?"

"We wanted to give you guys more time alone, and the rest is none of your business."

"Touchy, touchy. I think I hit a nerve." Juliane turned to Val and Carrie. "What do you guys think?"

Val nodded. "I think Juliane has you and Seth pegged. There's definitely something going on there."

"Quit bugging me about Seth."

"I have to have some payback, since you got me up so early." Juliane chuckled.

As they waited with the crowd for the penguins to appear, Elise wondered whether Juliane would keep bringing up Seth.

Elise didn't need more reminders that she still hadn't made a decision about letting him escort her to the wedding. With the wedding only a week away, she couldn't keep putting him off, but fear of making a mistake kept her from assessing the situation clearly.

"Here come the penguins." Carrie's observation rescued Elise from thoughts of Seth.

"Aren't they cute?" Juliane craned her neck to get a better look. "Look at the little girl who's leading the parade. She's precious."

"She sure is." Val nodded. "Eric and I will have to bring our kids to see this."

As they followed the crowd into the aquarium, Elise couldn't help thinking about how much fun Olivia would have leading the parade. Thoughts of the little girl brought another reminder of Seth. She didn't want to think about him now. She wanted to enjoy the day with her sister and cousins.

Elise poked Juliane in the ribs. "So are you in a better mood now?"

"Yeah. Sorry I was so grouchy. I'd never seen the penguin parade. The aquarium is super, and I love you for thinking about bringing me here." Juliane reached over and gave Elise a hug, then Val and Carrie, too.

"Okay, then. We're in for a fabulous day—aquarium, Ride the Ducks, dinner." Elise glanced at the brochure in her hand. "Looks like we start here with the World Rivers exhibit."

The foursome spent the morning in the aquarium where they took in a giant Pacific octopus, seahorses, alligators, fish from the Amazon River, a coral reef, frogs, a rainforest, jellyfish, sharks and a variety of other aquatic life.

"Next is Shark Central. You want to touch the sharks?" Carrie asked.

Juliane grimaced. "I think this is more for kids. I'll watch."

"I guess you really aren't as brave as I thought." Elise laughed.

"Remember, I told you I was a wimp."

While the sisters teased each other, Elise spied a dark-haired woman accompanied by two young boys. Elise nodded in their direction. "Is that Melanie Drake and her boys heading for the restaurant?"

Juliane turned. "Yeah. I'm so glad to see her getting out. I still can't imagine losing a husband at such a young age. Things have been tough for her since Tim's death. Let's go over and say hi."

"Okay." Elise looked over at Val and Carrie as Juliane took off toward Melanie. "You guys ready for lunch?"

"We are. Let's eat here since we're going more upscale tonight," Carrie said.

When Elise, Val and Carrie caught up to Juliane, she was already in conversation with Melanie.

"Why don't you join us for lunch?" Juliane asked.

Melanie shook her head slightly. "We don't want to intrude on your party."

"You're not intruding. We want you to join us."

Glancing at her boys, Melanie smiled. "Okay."

After they found seats and got their food, they took turns telling about their favorite exhibit.

Ryan, the older of the two boys, sat tall in his chair. "Touching the sharks was awesome! That was my favorite part."

"Andrew, what was your favorite?" Elise asked.

"I liked the underwater tunnels." Andrew glanced at Melanie. "Mom, can me and Ryan get a pretzel?"

Melanie knit her eyebrows. "Haven't you had enough to eat?"

"No," the boys chorused.

"Okay." Chuckling, Melanie gave them some money. "Be polite."

"We will." They raced off to get their pretzel.

"Sometimes they are a handful, and they're always hungry." Melanie looked over at Juliane. "I'm so sorry I'll miss the wedding, but I have to take the boys to see their grandparents."

"Wouldn't they understand if you came a different weekend?"

Melanie shook her head. "No. I didn't want to say anything with the boys here, but I know Tim's parents wouldn't forgive me if we didn't visit on the appointed weekend. They are very rigid about their schedules."

Juliane sighed. "That's too bad."

"I know." Melanie grimaced. "Even though I don't get along with Tim's parents that well, they still love their grandsons. I can't deny them the chance to see the boys. They grow up too fast. And I want the boys to have that connection to Tim."

Juliane patted Melanie's arm. "You know I've said this before. If you ever need anything, please let me know."

"Thanks." Melanie nodded. "One thing I've learned since Tim died so suddenly—you can't let an opportunity pass you by. I wish Tim and I had taken the time to bring the boys here before he died."

Ryan and Andrew scrambled back to the table, pretzels in hand, and the conversation took a different turn. But Melanie's statement hung in Elise's mind. Did it apply to her decision about Seth? He had nearly died in that accident. Was this second chance he was asking for something she should pursue? She wasn't going to find the answer unless she grabbed this occasion to explore the possibilities.

She was determined to face her apprehension and worry about Seth and accept his invitation. Life was too short to live in fear.

The chords of the wedding processional resonated through the church sanctuary. Family and friends who were there to share in Juliane and Lukas's special day filled the pews. Seth observed Lukas as he stood at the front, waiting for his bride. Seth wanted what Lukas had—a special love. And he was certain that his special love was Elise.

When Elise had agreed to be his date for the wedding, she'd given him some hope that they might find that love together.

Val and Carrie glided down the aisle toward the front, where Lukas, his father, grandfather and Nathan stood. Lukas smiled broadly as he waited for Juliane to appear. When Elise stepped into the doorway at the back, tenderness flooded Seth's heart. The stunning floor-length dress with the tiny straps was perfect for her statuesque figure. She stood silhouetted against the evening sunshine that flooded the church foyer, giving her an angelic appearance. When Elise walked past him on her way up the aisle, she turned for a second and smiled at him. More hope filled his heart.

Seth couldn't take his eyes off Elise. Even when everyone stood and turned to look at Juliane, Seth had his attention focused on Elise. Juliane finally came into Seth's line of vision. She was a beautiful bride, but all he could think of was seeing Elise as the bride holding her father's arm, walking down the aisle toward him. How could he make that happen? He knew one thing for certain. Patience was the key.

Seth wished he'd let love grow before Elise and he'd rushed into a relationship that had hurt both of them. He hadn't known about true love then. Finding the love of God in his own life had taught him how to love. Having Olivia had taught him about love, as well. Now he wanted to share that with Elise forever. He wanted to share a lasting love with her.

Seth's thoughts centered on Elise as he listened to the vows that Juliane and Lukas made to love and cherish each other. He hoped that one day he could make those same vows to Elise. Would his mistakes from the past make that dream impossible? He shook the question from his mind. Today was a day for love *and* hope.

After the ceremony, Seth waited for Elise while the photographer took photos of the wedding party and family. Seth enjoyed the laughter and camaraderie of the group. As he watched, he felt like part of the family, but he cautioned himself not to get ahead of reality. He was still on fragile ground where Elise was concerned. She'd only opened the door to her heart a sliver. He needed to wait for her to hand him the key to gain full access to her love.

When Elise's part of the photo session was finished, she walked back to where he was sitting in one of the pews. "Hi. Are you ready to go to the reception?"

Nodding, Seth grabbed his cane and stood. "I am. I haven't had a chance to tell you how fabulous you look in that dress."

"Thanks." She smiled as a hint of a blush colored her cheeks. "It's just a typical bridesmaid's dress."

"But you don't make any dress look typical."

"Now you've gone from compliments to flattery." She laughed and the sound warmed his heart.

"I'm only stating the truth. No flattery involved."

Elise reached out and tugged on the lapel of his dark gray suit. "You look pretty good yourself."

Seth's heart zinged. She'd touched him with no prompting—a good sign that she was feeling more comfortable around him. "Now whose using flattery?"

"Not me." She smiled at him with a feigned look of innocence. "Let's go."

Soft music played over the sound system in the all-purpose room at the recreation center. Seth saw the wisdom of the town fathers when they'd included this meeting space in their plans for the rec center. In the short time he'd been director he'd already seen the space used for parties and gatherings of all varieties. The facility served the residents of Kellerville well, and he was glad to be a part of this community. He wanted to find a permanent place here, with Elise by his side.

As they crossed the room, Elise took Seth's hand and guided him through the throng to one of the large, round tables near the front. He didn't even mind that she was leading him around. Her actions made his expectations grow. He reminded himself again that patience was the key.

"This is where we're sitting." Elise set her little blue purse on the chair in front of the place card with her name on it, then looked his way. "We get to sit with the bride and groom."

"Doesn't the maid of honor usually get to sit with the bride and groom?"

Elise nodded. "But Juliane had a lot of trouble deciding on the seating arrangement. We spent hours arranging and rearranging the seating chart. What a nightmare!"

"Why so much trouble?"

"Do you see this place?" She waved a hand in the air. "I think half the town is here. With our relatives, the people who work with Lukas and folks from church all being invited, this wedding is way too big for my tastes. Trying to decide who should sit where was like putting together a jigsaw puzzle. If you get married in this town, you have to have a gigantic wedding. If you leave someone off the guest list, you'll never hear the end of it. I think I'll elope when I get married."

Seth filed that bit of information away in the back of his brain. Had she said that to get his reaction? He wanted to make some witty quip about her letting him know before she decided to elope, but he figured he might be overstepping if he did. This was one time when he should keep his mouth shut. Besides, he shouldn't be guessing at her motives. He should steer the conversation into safer territory. "What are your duties during the reception?"

"Two big things are on the agenda during the reception. Sign the marriage license and give a toast." Elise chuckled. "I'm looking forward to the toast."

"So you have some good things to say about your sister?"

"I'm going to share some great stories."

"Will she still love you afterward?"

"Absolutely." Smiling, Elise motioned toward the door. "I see Val is making sure the guests have signed the guest book. Come with me while I mingle and make sure the guests know where they're supposed to sit, and I'll introduce you to some of the people you don't know."

"Sure. Sounds good!" Glad that Elise hadn't left him sitting at the table by himself, he followed her around the room like a lost puppy. He didn't even mind feeling that way. He enjoyed being with her and watching her interact with family and friends as they sampled the passed hors d'oeuvres.

She was like a brilliant diamond in a pile of ordinary rocks. Not only her beauty, but also her warm and caring manner sparkled and made everyone around her feel good, especially him. That's the way he'd felt from the moment he'd first met her, but he hadn't realized what a gem she was until he'd thrown it all away.

While Elise was parading Seth around the room, Juliane and Lukas arrived to a tumult of cheers. Elise and Juliane hugged, then followed Lukas, his dad and the minister to a corner of the room to sign the marriage license.

Extending his hand, Nathan joined Seth as he stood there watching the crowd. "Well, another good man bites the dust."

"Yeah." Shaking Nathan's hand, Seth laughed. "Hey, at least we gave him a great send-off at the bachelor party. And we saw a good ball game, too."

"Yeah, I love baseball. I enjoy working with the Little League."

"I appreciate your taking the time to coach. We have a lot of teams playing here at the rec center."

"Hey." Elise came up behind Seth and tapped him on the shoulder. "Let's sit down. They're ready to serve the meal."

"Sure." Seth escorted Elise to their table.

After the minister gave the blessing, the servers brought out the food. Soon everyone was enjoying the delicious entrees that Ray's cousin had supplied from his restaurant. Seth had a good time talking to Lukas's father, Niklas Frye, and his wife, Angela, as well as Lukas's grandfather, Ferd, and his friend Dot.

While they ate, Juliane and Elise conversed between themselves. With their heads close together, they laughed as if sharing a secret.

Lukas put his arm around Juliane. "Please share the joke. What's so funny?"

Juliane grimaced as she nodded toward the table next to them. "I just realized I stuck Nathan at a table where all the people are twice his age, but it's his own fault. I tried to convince him to bring a date, but he said he was too busy to find one."

"We've got to get him a girlfriend," Elise said.

"No, we don't." Juliane shook her head. "He doesn't have time for a girlfriend. He's in love with that bank. He spends all his time there. The only thing he does besides work is help with Little League a few months in the summer. He used to sing with the choir at church, but now he doesn't even do that. The bank takes top priority."

Seth glanced around the table. "Give him a break. He was my first volunteer when I sent out notices for volunteers to coach Little League."

Elise looked over at Seth. "Maybe you should help him find a girlfriend."

"Me?" Seth pointed to himself and gave Elise a wry smile. "I'm having enough trouble finding a girlfriend for myself."

"Well, if you look hard enough, you might find one right under your nose." Elise pretended to be angry, but he read the laughter and mischief in her eyes.

He leaned over and whispered in her ear. "Are you saying you're available?"

She whispered back, "I hope we can work on that."

Juliane poked Elise's arm. "No secrets, you two."

"I'm giving him a little advice on women." Elise grinned.

The jovial atmosphere and good-natured kidding continued as they finished their meal. When it came time for the toasts, Niklas Frye stood and told the crowd how proud he was to be there for his son. Dry eyes were hard to find after he finished giving the toast for his son and new daughter-in-law. Then Elise gave her toast amidst laughter, tears, applause and hugs.

Music, mirth and celebration continued to mark the rest of the evening. Seth had one of the best times of his life, not only because Elise was with him, but also because he felt as though he'd found a sense of belonging with these people. Olivia was the only thing missing, but he knew she wasn't ready to attend a wedding yet.

After Juliane and Lukas made their escape in their limousine, Seth and Elise lingered in the hall. The guests leisurely bid each other good-night as they made their way out to the parking lot. While Elise did her last duties as maid of honor, Seth checked to make sure the building maintenance supervisor had everything under control. When Seth escorted Elise to his pickup, the only people left in the building were the cleanup crew.

While Seth drove Elise to her house, she talked nonstop about the wedding and the reception. The joy in her voice wove its way into his heart. He wanted her to have that joy at her own wedding.

When she stopped talking, he glanced at her. "Now that Juliane is gone, are you going to feel strange living in the house all by yourself?"

"I don't know. I've been so busy I haven't had time to think about it." She peered at him in the darkened cab of his pickup. "Juliane put a lot of time into restoring that old house, so I was really surprised when she wanted to sell it to me."

Seth pulled into Elise's driveway. "Sometimes love makes a person do the unexpected."

"I'm beginning to see that." Opening her door, she slid out of the cab.

Seth stared after her. What had she meant by that comment? Was going out with him something she hadn't counted on doing? Grabbing his cane, he got out and hurried as fast as his cane would allow as he rushed to meet her on the other side of the pickup. "Thanks for letting me be your escort tonight."

"I'm glad you asked." A little smile curved her lips as she climbed the steps to her porch.

While she searched for her keys in her purse, he wondered what he should do now. Should he invite himself in? Should he try to kiss her good-night? He'd never been so indecisive about being with a woman in his life. He definitely wasn't going to shake her hand. Taking a cue from her was the best thing to do.

Producing the keys, she smiled at him. His heart raced. He wanted to kiss her.

She turned away and slipped the key into the lock. The door swung open, and she stepped inside. That pretty much told him he wasn't going to get that kiss. Patience. God was definitely teaching him patience.

"Thanks again. You helped make the evening very special. Good night." She started to close the door.

"Wait." If he'd made the evening so special, why was she afraid to let it last a little longer?

Startled, she looked back at him. "What?"

"Nathan asked me to go boating up at the lake this coming Saturday. He said I should ask you to come, too."

"Nathan's taking time away from the bank to go boating? I don't believe it."

Seth shrugged. "He said he wants to test some new gizmo for the boat that he plans to give his dad for Father's Day."

Elise narrowed her gaze. "Is this an invitation from you or him?"

"Does it make a difference?"

"Yes."

"I'm asking."

"Good. Then I accept." She smiled as she stood half hidden behind the door. "Would you, Olivia and Maggie like to join my folks and me for lunch after church next Sunday? It's Father's Day. I didn't know whether you had something special planned."

He wasn't going to get that kiss, but she was offering him more time with her even though they wouldn't be alone. Maybe she felt more comfortable that way. He had to give her time—that patience thing again. "Sounds great. Olivia will be thrilled."

"Give Olivia a kiss for me."

What about a kiss for me? The question nearly popped out of his mouth, but he smiled instead, his heart thudding. "I will. Good night."

Seth walked back to his pickup and got in. He sat there for a moment and thought about the evening, especially the ending. Elise's invitation for lunch on Father's Day was completely unexpected. Could she be falling for him after all?

Chapter Thirteen

Brilliant midmorning sunshine spilled through the kitchen window as Elise packed her bag for the day's outing with Seth and Nathan. With going to classes, filling out job applications and working at the store, Elise's week had been so busy that she hadn't had much time to think about Seth. Or about what the future might mean for them.

She shoved a tube of sunscreen into her bag. While she was taking a second accounting of its contents to make sure she hadn't forgotten anything, the doorbell rang.

Seth was here. Her stomach full of butterflies, she hurried to answer the door. When she flung it open, he stood there in jeans and a gray T-shirt advertising the Kellerville Recreation Center. He grinned, and she almost forgot to breathe. "Hi."

"You ready?"

"I am." She picked up her bag and slung it over her shoulder. "Aren't you going to get hot in those jeans?"

"Maybe, but I didn't want to scare anyone. The leg I broke is not a pretty sight." He chuckled as they walked to his pickup.

"No cane today? Does that mean you don't have to use one

anymore?" She hopped into the front seat and placed her bag at her feet.

"I've still got the cane with me, but I didn't need it to walk to your front door." He started the engine and backed out of her driveway.

"Are we picking up Nathan?"

"Nathan's not coming. He called and said he couldn't go boating. Something came up at the bank, and he has to be there to take care of it."

"Now, why doesn't that surprise me?" Elise straightened in her seat as the implications of Nathan's absence suddenly struck her. She was going to be spending the day alone with Seth. Her heart hammered as she swallowed the lump that had formed in her throat. "What are Olivia and your mom doing today?"

"They're on their way to Cincinnati to the zoo with a group from the rec center. So it's just you and me."

Still trying to calm her nerves, Elise fumbled with her seat belt. "Sounds like fun."

"I know you were looking forward to a day on the lake, but I thought we could go on a picnic up in the Hocking Hills instead. Someone at work told me about it. It takes about two hours to get there."

"I know. I've been there lots of times." Elise thought she heard a hopeful tone in his voice. He wanted her to agree to his suggestion. "I'd love to go."

"Great!"

As Seth drove out of town, Elise closed her eyes for a moment and took a deep breath. This was it—extended time for Seth and her to be alone together. She couldn't back out now. She had to take this chance to test her feelings.

"I looked up stuff online. The Ash Cave area looked interesting."

"It is. The whole area is fascinating. Perfect for all kinds of recreation."

"I figured we could eat lunch at the picnic area, then do a little hiking on the trails."

Elise jerked her head in his direction. "You obviously have no idea how hazardous parts of the trail are. How do you expect to hike with a cane?"

"Very slowly. Besides, I thought if I lost my balance, you'd be there to keep me from falling."

Elise released a harsh breath. "Will you quit kidding?"

"Who's kidding?" He grinned. "There are some easy trails there, too."

"Yeah, but you'll probably insist on doing the difficult part." Shaking her head, Elise narrowed her gaze as she looked at him.

"We'll see."

For several minutes they fell silent while Seth drove down the highway. Elise took in the rolling farmland on either side of the road. With the hum of the engine being the only thing that broke the silence, Elise worried that they had nothing to say to each other. Had they said everything that needed to be said?

The quiet didn't seem to bother Seth, but it made Elise worry that he wasn't enjoying their time together. Her worry just proved that she really did care about what he thought. She wanted to make things right between them. Did that mean she was falling in love with him again?

Maybe he didn't like to talk while he drove. He hadn't been very talkative during their ride out to the lake the other night. But this quiet Seth wasn't the Seth she used to know. He'd always been laughing and talking—the life of every party. Every once in a while these days she'd see that side of him, but rarely. Maybe everything he'd been through made him more serious.

"Have you heard from Juliane and Lukas?" Seth's question brought her thoughts to an abrupt halt.

"Juliane sent me an e-mail. They're having a marvelous time on their cruise. They're coming home tomorrow night. Since it's Father's Day, we're all going with Lukas's dad and grandfather to pick them up at the airport."

"Sounds like your family has a busy day planned tomorrow."

"Dad still insisted he have his usual lunch at the café for Father's Day, which always includes a big piece of German chocolate cake." She smiled at Seth. "And I'm glad he did, since you get to share it with us."

"I'm glad, too."

As the road began to wind through a forested area, Seth grew silent again. He turned on the CD player, and once again, the familiar guitar music floated through the air. For the rest of the drive, Elise enjoyed the scenery and tried to get used to the quiet companionship of the man who was ever so slowly winning her heart again.

Finally, they reached the turn off for Ash Cave. Seth pulled his pickup into a space in the parking lot, which was nearly full. He reached into the backseat and brought out a picnic basket. "Mom made us a picnic last night. We have way more food than we need because she thought we'd be having it on the boat with Nathan."

"That was so nice of her."

"She likes to pamper me, but she's been feeding me too much." Seth patted his stomach as he put the picnic basket on an empty table sitting among the trees. "She's always trying to fatten me up."

"You look fine to me."

Surprise showed in Seth's eyes as he laughed halfheartedly. "Thanks, but you haven't seen this leg, have you?"

"Well, no, and it seems from your description that I don't want to see it."

Seth laughed out loud as he took the food from the basket. "True."

Sitting next to him, Elise surveyed the sandwiches, potato salad, fruit salad and little cakes. "You're right. This is a lot of food."

As Seth settled beside her, he reached for her hand. "Let's pray."

Without saying anything, Elise put her hand in his and bowed her head. Instead of the prayer, all she could think of was how right she felt holding Seth's hand.

After the short prayer, he looked over at her. "Let's eat."

They ate in silence for a while, but Elise was getting used to Seth's new quiet way. While they ate, dozens of people laughed and talked as they walked through the area on their way to the trails.

Elise finished the last bite of her sandwich. "That was good. I'll have to write your mom and thank her."

"You can tell her in person tomorrow."

"I'll do that and send a note."

"If that's what you want to do." Seth shrugged.

"I do. Your mom deserves a lot of thanks for all she's done."

"That's for sure. She was such a big help with Olivia while I was on those crutches." Seth started putting the leftovers back into the basket. "I have her to thank for my faith, too. And that reminds me that we never finished that conversation we started about faith when we were at the Dairy Barn."

Elise nodded, wondering whether that was the thing Seth had been thinking about during the silence in the truck. "I remember. What about it?"

"You said something about God using even the bad stuff to do good."

"I believe He can do that."

"When you were talking about your family's Father's Day celebration, you got me to thinking about my dad."

Elise's heart sank. She hadn't been thinking, or she wouldn't have gone on and on about Father's Day. "I'm sorry. I wasn't very sensitive to the fact that you've lost your dad."

He gave her a wry smile. "Actually, I was thinking how his death and the heartbreaking circumstance made me examine my life."

"That's what I'm talking about. For years I tuned God out." She bit her lower lip. How could she tell Seth that breaking up with him had brought her back to God? She couldn't. "I've made so many mistakes, but I have to remember that nothing's impossible with God."

Seth smiled. "Thanks for reminding me, too."

"I think when we're going through stuff, we can't see how God could possibly use it for good. It's when we look back that we can see the good."

"Yeah, God sees the big picture that we can't see." Seth hopped up from the table. "Let's take the basket back to the pickup, then go for that hike."

By going very slowly, Seth managed to maneuver the trail circling the rim of the cave. Following close behind him, Elise watched every step to make sure he didn't fall. As they came down a long staircase near the end of the circle trail, Seth turned to Elise and grinned. "See? I told you I could go hiking."

Shaking her head, Elise smiled. "And I didn't even have to keep you from falling. So you proved me wrong. Let's go down the trail to the cave."

They walked through the narrow, quarter-mile gorge lined with hemlock and beech trees that gave way to the gigantic overhang of the recess cave formed from the erosion of the sandstone.

"Wow! You don't get the full picture until you see it for real." Seth put an arm around Elise's shoulders and drew her close.

"I always loved coming here when I was a kid. My parents, aunts, uncles and cousins used to come up here for weekend campouts." The pitter-patter of Elise's heart matched the sound of the water falling into the pool at the bottom of the cliff.

They watched the ribbons of water falling over the rim of the cliff where they'd walked earlier. Despite her accelerated heartbeat, somehow being with Seth today didn't set her emotions on edge. Instead, a contented feeling filtered through Elise's mind like the sunlight filtering through the trees to the floor of the cave. Looking up at him, she snuggled closer, and he smiled.

On the way back through the gorge, they walked arm-in-arm. They didn't talk, as if speaking would somehow ruin everything. Just before they reached the parking lot, a bridal party emerged from the picnic shelter and started making its way toward the path.

"A wedding." Elise placed a hand over her heart.

"You mean, they get married with hikers milling around?"

Elise nodded. "What are a few spectators when you can get married in a gorgeous setting like this?"

"So is this where you intend to do that eloping you were talking about at Juliane's wedding?"

For a moment, a picture of Seth and her holding hands and repeating vows while they stood in the cave near the waterfall flitted through her mind. Her pulse skittered. She didn't know how to answer. "I haven't thought about it."

"Maybe you should."

"Maybe." What did he mean by that? Was he implying that she should get prepared to elope, or did he just mean she should consider this particular spot? At one time, she had very much wanted to marry Seth. Was she confusing the past with the present?

She was definitely testing her feelings today, but rather than answers, more questions emerged.

Could she trust herself to love him again? Would they be good for each other? Was this what God wanted for them? How was she supposed to find the answers for these questions? When would she have a clear understanding?

On Father's Day, as soon as church was over, Seth couldn't hold Olivia back. She darted out of the pew before he could stop her. He glanced up to see Elise coming their way. He knew trying to catch his daughter was a lost cause.

Watching Olivia race toward Elise, he could almost see himself doing the same thing, if it weren't for the cane. He was as eager as Olivia to see Elise. Yesterday had been a taste of everything he wanted for the future. He wanted to make the most of the time he would spend with her today.

Olivia raced up to greet Elise. "Hi, 'Lise."

Smiling at him over the top of Olivia's head, Elise reached down and picked Olivia up. "Did you give your daddy a big kiss and hug for Father's Day?"

Olivia's curls bobbed as she nodded her head and shoved a folded-up paper at Elise. "I bringed you this."

"Thank you. I'm getting a very nice collection on my refrigerator, but I'm running out of room. I think we'll have to start a scrapbook for all of your pictures." Still holding Olivia, Elise carefully unfolded the paper with one hand and revealed Olivia's Sunday school paper, showing a picture of Joseph and his coat of many colors. Elise set Olivia on the floor and refolded the paper before putting it in her purse. "Are you ready for lunch?"

"Yes." Olivia jumped up and down and clapped her hands. "Chicken finners."

"I like those, too." Elise laughed, then looked at Seth. "What about you?"

Just watching my two favorite females. He wanted to say that, but he wasn't sure how Elise would take the comment, even after the things they'd shared yesterday. "I'm not sure what I'm going to eat."

"Chicken finners, Daddy."

Seth ruffled Olivia's curls. "Will you give me a taste of yours?"

"I give you lots." Nodding, Olivia took his hand.

His daughter's tiny hand resting in his filled his heart to overflowing with love. God had allowed him to have this child. He was so thankful he'd come to find the faith and forgiveness that had sent him in search of Olivia. He couldn't imagine his life without her. Father's Day made him that much more aware of his blessings.

He turned to Elise. He couldn't imagine his life without her, either. "Would you like to ride with us?"

Elise slipped her arm through his. "Okay."

With a beautiful and talented woman on one arm and his daughter's hand in his, he felt like the luckiest man in the world. Everything in his life was looking good.

On this Father's Day—his first one with Olivia—he realized he'd almost missed knowing his daughter. The thought made him more grateful than ever that finding faith in God had changed his life. The thought that he may never have known Olivia made him heartsick. But, thanks to God, she made his life wonderful.

When they got to the car, Seth buckled Olivia into her car seat. Maggie hopped into the back, leaving Elise to sit up front with him. He wondered whether his mother had sat in the back because she wanted to be with Olivia or because she was trying to make sure Elise would sit in front with him.

Olivia's sweet little voice, jabbering in toddler talk, sounded through the cab of Seth's pickup truck. Elise caught his eye and smiled. With a slight nod, he acknowledged her smile. Things were falling into place with Elise, but he still had to remind himself against looking too far into the future. He should enjoy the day and leave the future in God's hands.

When they arrived at the café, Elise's parents met them at the door. As they entered, the café hummed with after-church diners. The hostess showed their group to a booth. Seth didn't miss the way Elise's parents and his mother did little to disguise their intent to have him and Elise sitting together. He had to stifle a laugh when Olivia thwarted their plans by sitting in between Elise and him.

But even Olivia's innocent wish to sit by Elise had Seth thinking about the three of them as a family. He could imagine sharing meals like this all of the time, not only with Elise and Olivia but with Ray and Barbara, as well. They talked about the upcoming Fourth of July festivities and about Juliane and Lukas's expected return from their honeymoon.

When they'd finished eating, Seth turned to Maggie. "Elise and I are going to take Olivia over to the park. We'll walk home afterward. So you can drive home. We'll walk home, or Elise will give us a ride."

Maggie narrowed her gaze. "Are you sure you should be walking home on that leg?"

"Absolutely. I need the exercise, especially after the meal we just ate. Walking will help strengthen my leg."

"Okay, if you say so." Maggie shrugged.

When they left the café, Seth and Elise bid goodbye to their parents and set off for the park a few blocks away. For a couple of blocks, they walked without saying much. Olivia walked between Seth and Elise as they each held one of her hands.

They looked like a family. They felt like a family. Could they be a family?

Seth cautioned himself to be patient once again. Elise's willingness to have him as an escort to the wedding, today's invitation for lunch and their outing yesterday all spelled good things for the future. But he had to remind himself not to rush things.

"I'm so excited Juliane and Lukas are coming home tonight. I'm so glad their wedding and reception were everything she had planned. I thought the way they set up Dot and his grandfather to catch the bouquet and the garter was so cute." Elise's statement brought him back to reality.

"Isn't the maid of honor supposed to catch the bouquet?"

"That's only if the maid of honor is looking to be the next bride."

"Is that so?" That probably meant Elise wasn't looking to be the next bride. He should have guessed that from her blasé reaction to his suggestion that she elope and have a wedding at Ash Cave. Her statement ought to put his overactive thoughts in check.

"Dot and Ferd are adorable together. I wouldn't be surprised if they get married soon."

"I enjoyed getting to know them better. I had no idea Lukas's parents and grandfather had escaped from East Germany."

"Yes, that was quite a story." Elise sighed. "I'm so glad Lukas came into Juliane's life. If it hadn't been for Lukas, my dad may never have gotten the help he needs. Dad and Lukas are very committed to their addiction recovery group."

Seth wondered whether Elise was glad he'd come into her life again. Did she finally see him as an asset? He was afraid she might still see him as a liability. So far she seemed to have done all the giving, and he'd done all the taking. He wanted to make her life better. How could he do that? "They have a wonderful ministry."

"I know." Unshed tears sparkled in Elise's eyes. Blinking them away, she cleared her throat. "How long is your mom going to stay?"

"At least through the Fourth of July." Seth lifted his cane. "I think as soon as the doc says I can quit using this, she'll feel like she can leave. She could hardly wait until school was done so she could come back and take care of us."

"Olivia will miss her."

"I know. I wish I could talk her into moving here. She could retire if she wanted to, but she tells me she doesn't want to leave her friends and family in Pittsburgh."

"Change can be difficult."

Is that why you're not quite convinced of the changes I've tried to make? Seth wished he could ask that question. He still sensed a barrier between them. One he couldn't break through. He wasn't sure what to say. They weren't talking about him, anyway. They were talking about his mother, so he should keep the focus on her. "We'll see whether she changes her mind."

"Swings, Daddy." Letting go of their hands, Olivia pointed, then raced ahead to the playground.

Accompanied by watchful adults, a dozen other children played on the swings, slide and jungle gym. Shrieks of laughter filled the air.

Waving his cane in the air, Seth looked over at Elise. "This thing is slowing me down. Will you catch her before she tries to get in a swing by herself and falls down?"

"Sure." Elise jogged ahead and helped Olivia into the swing.

By the time Seth caught up to them, Elise was pushing Olivia in one of the toddler swings. "Hi, Daddy. I go high."

"I see. Are you having a good time?"

Nodding, Olivia giggled, and Seth's heart melted. Seth and Elise took turns pushing the swing as Olivia begged to go higher each time. When she finally grew tired of swinging, she charged over to the slide and jungle gym and joined the other children playing there.

When Olivia got ready to go down the slide, she waved. "'Lise, watch me."

"Okay. I'm watching."

Olivia came down the slide and threw her hands in the air when she finished.

"That was good." Elise smiled at Olivia.

"I go again." Olivia scampered back to the steps going up to the slide.

Seth motioned toward an area where several other adults were watching children. "Let's go sit on that bench over there while we watch her."

"Sure."

Seth sat next to Elise on the bench under the big oak tree. Every time Olivia was ready to go down the slide, she would call to Elise. Seth didn't miss Elise's wistful expression as she watched his daughter. What was Elise thinking?

"You are blessed to have that little girl."

"I know." Was that what put the wistful look on Elise's face? He wanted to tell her that she blessed his life, too, but this wasn't the time or place.

Olivia raced and climbed and laughed with the other children. Seth figured she'd keep going until she dropped unless he told her that they had to leave.

Elise leaned closer to him. "Do you think she'll ever wear out?"

Chuckling, Seth tried to keep his focus on Olivia rather than on Elise's nearness. "I was thinking the same thing. What do you think will happen if I say we have to leave?"

Elise touched his arm. "You may have to bribe her."

Trying not to read anything into her touch, Seth chuckled

again as he stood. "I'm going to make my move and see how we fare."

"Good luck." Elise went with him as he approached the slide.

"Olivia, it's time to go."

Olivia looked up at him. "No. More slide."

"Okay, one more slide, then we go."

Olivia raced to the slide and went down, then started to go back again. Seth tried to reach to her, but she scooted by him. Elise ran after Olivia and picked her up. She squirmed, but Elise held on tight and whispered something in Olivia's ear. The little girl stopped resisting and nodded her head. Seth could hardly wait to find out what Elise had said to his daughter.

On the walk back to Seth's house, Olivia gave out halfway, and Elise had to carry the little girl. She fell asleep in Elise's arms. When they reached the house, Elise carried Olivia inside. Seth led the way back to her room. After Elise laid the sleeping child on her bed, Seth stood beside Elise and watched Olivia sleep for a few moments.

Seth whispered, "Let's go."

Elise nodded and followed him to the living room. "I think she wore herself out."

"Thanks for your help. Can you stay?" He hoped she'd say yes.

She glanced at her watch, then back at him. "Okay. For a little while."

Seth plopped onto the couch and motioned for Elise to join him. "What did you say to Olivia back at the park?"

"I told her this was a special day for daddies and that she should do what you said." Elise smiled. "That little girl adores you."

"And I adore her. I never imagined how great being a dad

could be." Seth's heart thrummed. He adored Elise, too. He wished she felt the same way.

Elise jumped up and rummaged through her oversized purse. She pulled out a box and handed it to Seth. "I almost forgot to leave this with you."

"What is it?" Seth examined the box covered in paper with pink scribbles all over it.

"Olivia's Father's Day gift for you. My cousin Val told me about this, so I took Olivia along when Val took her kids."

Seth knit his brow. "Am I supposed to open this now?"

Elise bit her bottom lip, then grimaced. "I was going to have you open this with Olivia, but she fell asleep."

"Should I wait?"

"Probably, but I want to see how you like it. The lid comes off without ruining the wrapping paper, so you can put it back on and open it again with Olivia later. She made the wrapping paper, too."

"I can tell." Seth lifted the lid to reveal a small plate imprinted with two little handprints surrounded by flowers. Olivia's name and age were written at the bottom.

"Do you like it?"

"Absolutely. This is so special. Thank you." He laid the plate aside. He wanted to kiss her. He'd wanted to kiss her for weeks, but he'd held himself back. Not today. "Unless you tell me no, I'm going to kiss you."

When Elise made no protest, he pulled her into his arms. He kissed her, then held her close. Kissing her and holding her was like coming home. He never wanted to leave. Finally, he held her at arms' length. "I want you in my life. Not just today, but forever. Can we work on that?"

Nodding, Elise closed her eyes, and Seth kissed her again. With God's help, Seth was determined to make their love work this time.

Chapter Fourteen

On the Fourth of July, Elise had a spring in her step as she walked down her street on her way to Seth's place. Houses on every block sported flags and patriotic banners. She looked forward to riding in the parade on the church float. Hours of practice on the songs with Seth had brought the two of them even closer. Father's Day had been a turning point for them. Her decision to let Seth back into her life brightened every day. Today was another day to show Seth that the past was forgotten, and she was looking to the future.

When she reached Seth's house, he was sitting on the front steps. Olivia peddled madly while she rode her tricycle back and forth on the porch. Red, white and blue streamers trailed from the handlebars and seat, and one little flag fluttered from the handlebar support.

When Seth saw Elise, he jumped up and met her halfway down the walk. He pulled her into his arms and kissed her soundly. "Happy Fourth of July."

Her heart soaring like fireworks, Elise held him close for a moment, then looked up at him as they stood in each other's arms. "Happy Fourth to you, too. I see Olivia's all decked out for the parade."

Draping one arm around Elise's shoulders, Seth turned to look at his little girl, who was still riding her tricycle. "She is overexcited about today. This'll be her first parade."

"Are you planning to let her ride in the children's parade?"

"She is. Mom helped her decorate her tricycle this morning."

"Who's walking with her? You or your mom?"

Seth chuckled. "Mom. She says that way I can take pictures."

"Makes sense." Elise glanced toward the house. "Where *is* your mom?"

"She'll be out in a minute. Then we'll go."

Looking in Elise's direction, Olivia stopped her tricycle. Dressed for the day in her red, white and blue gingham sundress, she hopped off and raced to meet Elise. "'Lise, we go to parade."

"I know." Elise hunkered down next to the little girl. "Where'd you get that pretty dress?"

"Gramma gots it for me."

Standing, Elise glanced up at Maggie as she stepped onto the porch. "Hi, Maggie. Where'd you find Olivia's cute dress?"

"My sister Susan sent it. Isn't it perfect for the Fourth of July?" Maggie held her arms out as she displayed her shirt dotted with red, white and blue stars. "I'm all decked out in my patriotic colors, too. A little crazy, but fun."

"You're right in line with the rest of the town. Wait until you see the decorations on Main Street," Elise replied.

"Let's head to town and see them." Seth grabbed Olivia's tricycle and brought it down to the sidewalk, then picked up the cane lying against the step.

Elise looked at him with a frown. "You told me you were done with the cane."

"I am, but I'm going to use it to push Olivia on her tricycle. I figure there's no way she's going to make it all the way to town without getting tired, and I certainly can't ride that tricycle." Seth put the end of the cane at the back of the trike and pushed. "See how it works?"

Elise laughed. "You are clever."

"You're just now figuring that out?"

Shaking her head, Elise rolled her eyes. "You mean, I was supposed to have known this?"

Seth put an arm around her waist and pulled her close, then whispered, "I was clever enough to fall for you."

Elise didn't say anything, just smiled up at him while she let the wonder of their renewed relationship seep into her soul. Why had she let weeks pass before she believed Seth had changed? She'd wasted so much time worrying about the past instead of looking at the present, and the man who'd shown her over and over how much he'd changed.

The foursome made a little parade of their own as they traveled the four-block distance to town. Elise enjoyed the walk as she soaked up the flavor and excitement of the day. The Fourth of July always found Kellerville decked out in red, white and blue streamers and balloons. American flags graced every corner. Red, white and blue banners and flags decorated the clock tower and gazebo in the square. The whole town had turned out to celebrate.

The aroma of hot dogs, hamburgers, french fries and various other culinary delights came from the booths lining the streets. Picnic tables dotted the square. A band was setting up their equipment on a platform in front of the courthouse while folks gathered along the streets in anticipation of the parade.

Seth helped Olivia and his mom find a perfect spot for viewing the parade. "We'll meet you right here when the parade is over."

Elise picked up Olivia. "Watch for us, and wave to your daddy and me when we go by, okay?"

"I will." Olivia waved her little flag as Elise gave her a hug and set her down.

Seth gave his cane to his mom. "You might need this to push her trike in the kids' parade after we eat. So I'll leave it with you."

Laughing, Maggie took the cane. "We'll see you later."

Elise put her hand in Seth's as they hurried the two short blocks to the church, where they planned to change. When they arrived, Juliane was in her Statue of Liberty costume and Lukas was dressed as Uncle Sam.

Juliane rushed up to them. "Your costumes are hanging on the rack just inside the door. What took you guys so long to get here?"

"Had to get Olivia and my mom a good spot to watch the parade." Seth motioned back toward town.

Elise grimaced. "We'll hurry."

"Come on." Seth grabbed Elise's hand and they raced to the church.

Once inside, he stole a quick kiss before they went their separate ways to change. While Elise changed, she contemplated the love that was growing in her heart for Seth. She was beginning to believe he'd proved himself as a man she could love and trust with her heart.

Minutes later, Elise emerged from the church building dressed as Dolly Madison, and Seth soon followed in his Minuteman costume. They joined Juliane and Lukas on the float.

Lukas handed them their mikes. "We've already tested all the sound equipment. Everything's good to go."

"Thanks." Seth took his spot on the float next to Elise.

An hour later the float came to a stop in the church parking lot. Seth helped Elise down from the platform. "That was fun. I hope we can do that again next year."

Elise grinned. "And Olivia was beside herself when she finally recognized you in your costume. Do you want to stay in the costumes, so Olivia can see us again, or do you think we'll get too hot?"

"Olivia will get a kick out of it."

"We can change into our other clothes later at the store if we want."

"Sounds like a good plan to me." Grabbing Elise's hand, Seth turned to Juliane and Lukas. "Let's head down to the town square. We'll find my mom and Olivia, then get something to eat."

"I'm ready for food." Lukas adjusted his hat.

"Okay, Uncle Sam, let's go eat." Juliane kissed him on the cheek.

"Lead the way." Chuckling, Lukas took her hand.

The two couples made their way through the crowd that still lingered along the parade route. Seth called his mom on his cell phone to let her know they were on their way.

When they reached the square, where the crowd was even larger, Elise spied Olivia and Maggie and pointed in their direction. "There they are waiting right where we left them."

Olivia ran to greet them. "I see'd you in the prade."

Seth scooped Olivia up in his arms. "Did you have fun?"

Olivia nodded. "We eat now?"

"That's the plan. Then your parade."

After the group bought food and found a picnic table, they enjoyed a leisurely lunch. Barbara and Ray joined them. After lunch, the adults cheered on the participants in the children's parade. Olivia hammed it up for the crowd as she peddled her trike around the square with the other children. The rest of the afternoon sped by as they listened to the bluegrass band playing patriotic songs. Everyone enjoyed the music while they relaxed under the tulip poplars and buckeye trees shading the square.

Elise relished this time, surrounded by the people she loved and the goodness of her hometown. More and more she thought about Seth and Olivia in terms of family. She had to tell Seth how she felt in no uncertain terms.

Seth whistled as he straightened his desk. The past few weeks had been the best times of his life. Everything he'd hoped for was falling into place. He loved his job. Olivia had settled into her day-care routine now that his mom had returned to Pittsburgh to get ready for another school year. Best of all, Elise had opened her heart and let him walk back in. She'd told him she'd moved beyond the past while they watched the Fourth of July fireworks. She loved him. Nothing could top that.

Elise, Olivia and he often ate their evening meal together. Elise's parents watched Olivia when Elise and he went out with Juliane and Lukas. Their excursion back to Hocking Hills for a canoe trip reminded Seth of the wedding they'd seen there. He wanted more than ever to make Elise his bride. Her graduation party was coming up in two weeks, and Seth planned to ask Elise to marry him.

Grabbing the stack of mail on his desk, he sorted through the envelopes. One envelope jumped out at him. The letter had been forwarded from his old address in Pittsburgh. When he read the return address on the envelope, his stomach sank— Sophie Conrad. The return address indicated that she was living in Atlanta. Why was Sophie sending him a letter? He ripped it open.

Dear Seth,

I hope this letter finds you. I tried to call you, but the

number I had was disconnected. My life has changed, and I realize I made a big mistake when I signed away my parental rights to Olivia. I know I have no legal standing, but I hope you can find it in your heart to let me see her. I know I can't get my parental rights back. I'm only asking to see her. Is there any chance that we can get together to discuss this? If you say no, I will certainly understand, but I'm begging for a chance. I want desperately to see my little girl.

Sophie

Seth crumpled the letter in his hand, then threw it on the desk. He didn't want to deal with Sophie or her request, but as a Christian, he knew he should put himself in her shoes. How would he want to be treated if he were in her place? As he answered that question, he realized he had no choice but to see what she had to say. Yes, she'd given up her rights, but he understood what it meant to make a bad decision and regret it later.

What would happen if Elise found out? What would she think? How would Sophie's reappearance affect his and Elise's relationship? Maybe he shouldn't tell her about this initial meeting. If nothing came of it, she would never have to know.

But how would all of this affect Olivia? Would she be confused about the mother she probably didn't remember suddenly coming back into her life?

The questions pummeled his mind and gave him a headache. Plopping onto his chair, he put his head in his hands. What was he going to do? He couldn't tell Elise until he'd met and talked with Sophie first. Then he would try to explain everything and pray that she could understand and accept his decision.

Seth picked up the crumpled letter and smoothed it out on

his desk. As Seth punched out the phone number Sophie had written at the bottom of her letter, he hoped for the best.

A week later, Elise rushed into the rec center and headed for Seth's office. She had to share her good news. She had job! When she reached the outer office where his assistant worked, the desk was empty. So Elise tapped lightly on the door, then slowly opened it.

Elise's heart plummeted as she observed the scene before her. Seth stood by his desk, and a woman with long dark hair had her arms around his neck. As Elise was about to turn and run, Seth looked her way. Immediately, he extracted himself from the woman's arms. "Elise."

The woman turned. Sophie.

Elise couldn't make her legs move. She stood glued to the floor. As she looked at Seth, she tried to keep her lips from quivering. She wanted to ask what was going on here, but she couldn't form a coherent sentence, even in her mind.

Her dark eyes wide, Sophie looked from Elise back to Seth. While Elise grasped for some explanation, Sophie muttered her thanks to Seth and fled from the room.

Seth immediately went to the door and closed it behind her. "Elise, let me explain."

Elise was still too stunned to protest. He led her to a chair and pulled his beside hers. She fought to control her emotions. She didn't want to cry in front of Seth. "Why were you hugging her?"

"She was hugging *me,* not the other way around. She was thanking me for agreeing to let her see Olivia."

Elise frowned. "You're letting her see Olivia? What are you talking about?"

Seth proceeded to explain Sophie's request and his decision to grant it. As Elise listened to his explanation, her apprehension grew.

Elise took a shaky breath while anger and hurt welled up inside her. "Why would you keep this from me?"

"I felt that I needed to talk to her first and gauge her sincerity, her state of mind. I didn't want to introduce her into all of my life here until I was sure she was being honest with me about the contact she was seeking. I want the best for Olivia."

"What about the best for us?"

"Sophie's relationship with Olivia has nothing to do with us."

Elise shook her head. "If you think that, then you're not thinking clearly. Whatever involves Olivia will have an impact on all of us. How can this not affect our relationship?"

Seth appeared at a loss. "Please understand. I love you. This thing with Sophie doesn't change that."

Elise closed her eyes against the troubled feelings that swamped her. Shaking her head, she put her hands over her face. Seth put his arm around her shoulders, and she moved away. "I can't think when you touch me."

Seth immediately dropped his arm. "Please don't shut me out."

Finally looking at him, Elise straightened her shoulders. "I need some time to think about this. I'm not sure how to deal with it. I need some space."

"Okay. If that's what you need. When you finally make up your mind, I'll be here, waiting for you."

"Goodbye, Seth." Standing, Elise gathered all her dignity as she left the room.

Elise walked calmly through the reception area. As soon as she was out of Seth's sight, she sprinted to her car. The numbness that shock had brought was fading. She wanted it back. Then maybe this whole thing wouldn't hurt so much.

While she drove home, the confusion about Seth returned with a vengeance. How was she supposed to know what to do?

Was she being selfish? Maybe. But she couldn't go forward with their relationship until she could deal honestly with her feelings about Sophie, Olivia and Seth.

Elise knew Olivia deserved to know her mother. It was good that Sophie wanted to have a part in her daughter's life. But Elise wasn't sure how that would affect her. She had to be sure she could handle these tangled relationships in Seth's life. If she was going to be a permanent part of his life, Sophie would be coming and going, too. Elise had to square this in her own mind and heart. She also had to deal with the fact that even though Seth said he loved her, he'd kept this from her. How could they have love without trust?

After Elise pulled her car into the garage, she leaned on the steering wheel and cried. She cried for the hurt and misery in her heart, and she cried for Olivia and Sophie. In all the disheartening events, Elise hadn't told Seth about her job. What did it matter now that she'd been offered a teaching position in Kellerville?

How could they resolve this situation? Elise didn't see any answers, even from God.

Chapter Fifteen

As Seth carried Olivia into the church fellowship hall, he saw Elise, Juliane, Barbara and several other women working in the church kitchen. Elise's laughter echoed through the empty hall. The sound broke his heart. She was happy without him. He wanted to make her happy, but he'd done nothing but bring her pain. Why had he messed up again?

Her graduation party would start in about an hour. Elise probably wouldn't welcome him, even though her parents had sent him an invitation. He wanted to celebrate with her, but he'd told her he'd give her space. So he'd drop off his gift and leave. Although leaving would hurt, he didn't want his presence to ruin her very important day.

With an ache filling his chest, he stopped near the doorway and set Olivia on the floor. He held Elise's card in one hand while he held Olivia's hand in the other. As he observed the banners and streamers decorating the hall, Elise walked out of the kitchen.

Instantly, Olivia escaped from his grasp and ran across the room to Elise. "'Lise, we bringed you present."

Reaching down, Elise smiled and picked up Olivia. "That's very nice of you."

Olivia pointed in his direction. "Daddy gots it."

Elise looked up and met his gaze. As she walked toward him, her smile disappeared, and he read the sadness in her eyes.

A huge weight seemed to be crushing the air out of his lungs, but he took a step forward. "Hi, Elise."

"Daddy, gib 'Lise present." Squirming to get down again, Olivia reached out her hand, oblivious to the discomfort brewing between the two adults.

Elise put Olivia down, and she scampered to meet him. Seth handed the card to Olivia. Could his little girl smooth the way for him? He wished she could, but he couldn't use his child to gain access to Elise's heart. He had to stand on his own. This time he was putting everything in God's hands—something he'd forgotten to do when faced with Sophie's letter.

Olivia raced back to Elise and handed it to her. "Open."

Elise hunkered down beside Olivia. "Will you help me?"

Nodding, Olivia tore open the envelope. Elise pulled out the card and opened it.

Seth held his breath.

Would the simple poem inside convey to her how proud he was of her accomplishment? He wanted her to know he was sorry. He wanted to say these things out loud and beg her to take him back, but he had to honor her request to give her space.

As Elise read the card, Seth couldn't decipher her reaction. She never looked his way but continued to share the card with Olivia. Elise pulled a folded paper from the envelope and unfolded it. A smile crept across her face as she examined the paper.

"I love your drawing. I'll put it with all of your others." She gave Olivia a hug. "Thank you."

"See more." Olivia pulled a smaller envelope out of the bigger one and shoved it at Elise.

Elise opened the flap and pulled out the tickets. She shuffled through them, then stood as she finally glanced his way. She took Olivia's hand and slowly walked toward him.

Olivia danced around them as Elise stopped in front of him. Tightness around her mouth indicated a forced smile, but at least she'd made the effort.

"Thank you." Shaking her head, she spread the tickets in her hand. "I can't believe you did this. How'd you know I wanted to see these plays?"

"I know how much you love musicals. Two tickets for each, so you can take a friend." His heart hammering, he wished he were that friend, but he couldn't say so.

"I hope you enjoy them, and I hope you have a wonderful party tonight. Congratulations on your graduation and your job." Seth picked up Olivia. "I just wanted to drop that by. We'll be going now."

"Thanks for stopping." She stared at him as if she were going to say something else, but she remained silent.

"You're welcome." With an aching heart, he knew she wasn't going to ask him to stay.

Seth turned toward the door, and thankfully, Olivia didn't complain. He'd promised to get her ice cream on the way home, so she wouldn't make a fuss about leaving. Could he drown his own sorrows in ice cream? No. He had to live with his mistakes, face the consequences of his actions and find the answer about his future that God would provide.

On the Sunday before Labor Day, Elise's mother cornered her as she was leaving church. Barbara gave Elise one of her no-nonsense looks. "I know you and Seth have had a falling out—"

"I don't want to talk about Seth."

"I'm not going to ask you about Seth, but I want you to come over to Seth's this afternoon while I'm watching Olivia.

He's golfing with your dad and Lukas this afternoon, so he won't be there. You don't have to worry about any awkward meetings or conversations. You can help me bake chocolate chip cookies and some pies for the Labor Day picnic."

"Why are you baking at his house? Why not watch Olivia at yours?"

"It's easier to transport some groceries and a few baking utensils than Olivia's toys."

Sighing, Elise knew agreeing to go was easier than arguing with her mom. "Okay, I'll meet you there."

The trouble with Seth was in the forefront of Elise's mind as she parked in front of his house. She hadn't been here since before the incident with Sophie. She didn't know how she'd handle being in his house, but she wanted to spend more time with Olivia. This was the perfect chance, since Seth wouldn't be present.

When Elise walked into the kitchen, her mom had already prepared Olivia a sandwich. The child was sitting in her little table while she ate. When she saw Elise, Olivia jumped up and grabbed Elise's hand and pulled her toward the table. "'Lise, eat here."

"I'm not sure I'll fit at your table."

"'Lise, sit with me, please?" Olivia continued to pull on Elise's hand.

Elise laughed as she looked at the tiny chair, then at her mom. "Do you think I can possibly fit my long legs under that table?"

Barbara chuckled. "I kind of doubt it. Your knees will be under your chin, but I'll sit there, too, if that helps."

Barbara made sandwiches for herself and Elise, then joined Elise and Olivia. Despite the less-than-comfortable seating arrangement, Elise enjoyed every minute of her time with Olivia. Sadness surrounded her heart as she remembered all the times she'd shared with Seth and Olivia. She missed the little girl, but she couldn't make a decision about Seth based on Olivia alone.

After lunch, Elise and Barbara made the cookies while Olivia played in her little kitchen. Pretending to bake cookies, Olivia kept showing them samples. Olivia's sweet presence made Elise ache for the way things used to be. She yearned to turn back the clock.

The hurt from Seth's decision not to tell her about Sophie from the beginning still lingered. His actions had diminished her trust in him. On the other hand, Elise couldn't forget his graduation gift. His thoughtfulness had softened her heart. She'd almost asked him to stay for the party, but she'd forced herself to keep her distance until she'd really worked through this whole thing.

While Elise's mind rolled the thoughts over and over, Barbara's cell phone rang. Elise continued to work while her mother took the call. After Barbara shut off her phone, her words tumbled over each other, and Elise couldn't understand what her mom was saying.

"Mom, please slow down and start over. What's the problem?"

"It's your grandfather. He's fallen, and your grandmother isn't strong enough to help him up."

"I can go."

Barbara shook her head. "They want me to come. Besides, I want to take this time to talk to them about moving to an assisted living place. I've been trying to talk them into it for months. I think this incident may convince them that it's time." Barbara touched Elise's arm. "Please stay with Olivia."

Elise hugged her mom. "Okay. Tell Grandpa and Grandma I'm praying for them."

After Barbara hurried from the house, Olivia played quietly in the corner of the kitchen with her little table and chairs and toy kitchen set. The timer sounded and Elise took the cookies from the oven. She put in a new batch, then started to peel and slice peaches for pie. Then she made the dough for piecrusts.

Thankfully, her mother hadn't pressed for answers about Elise's disagreement with Seth. But as she worked, Elise wondered if it might be good for her to have to answer some tough questions. Was she doing the same thing again that she'd done when she first came home—refusing to talk things out? This time even Juliane hadn't pressed her to talk about it.

While she rolled the pie dough, her mind wrapped around the fact that she would be here by herself to deal with Seth when he returned. How was she going to handle that? What would he say? Why did life have to be so full of uneasy decisions?

As Elise laid a crust in a pie plate and poured the peaches into it, her cell phone rang. She answered it. "Mom, is Grandpa okay?"

"Everything's fine, but I'm going to be here for a while. Are you good with watching Olivia until Seth comes home?"

"Yes. Thanks for calling. Talk to you later." Elise wasn't ready to deal with Seth, but Olivia needed her. She'd been praying about this decision. Was her inevitable meeting with Seth today part of that answer?

Elise put her cell phone on the counter. After she put another batch of cookies in the oven, she glanced over to the corner where Olivia was playing, but she wasn't there. Elise's heart jumped into her throat. Where had the little girl gone?

Elise ran to the living room. "Olivia, where are you? Olivia?"

No answer.

Elise raced through the house, calling Olivia's name. Still no answer. Had she gone out of the house and wandered away? Elise didn't want to think about the possibility. Frantic, she ran into the yard and called. There was no sign of the little girl. Elise took a calming breath. Panic was going to get her nowhere. *Lord, please keep Olivia safe and help me find her.*

With a sense of peace filling her heart, Elise returned to the kitchen and looked around. God would help her. She had to put herself in the mind of a little girl. Where would she go? Walking slowly through the house, Elise looked in every corner and closet and under every bed. Still no Olivia. Her heart pounding with fear, Elise stopped and covered her mouth with a hand in order to hold back a sob. She had to find Olivia. *Please, Lord.*

When Elise glanced up, Seth was standing in the doorway. He stepped toward her, concern in his eyes. "What's wrong? What are you doing here?"

Her pulse pounding, she wasn't sure she could speak and not let go of that sob. How was she going to explain that she'd lost Olivia? Closing her eyes, she couldn't bear to look at him. "I'm watching Olivia because my grandfather fell and my mom went to help. And Olivia's missing. I…"

The sob escaped. Elise leaned against the wall and put her head in her hands.

"It's going to be all right, Elise. We'll find her." Seth gathered Elise in his arms, and she didn't resist. "Where have you looked?"

"Everywhere." Not feeling she deserved his reassurance, Elise took a shaky breath and stepped away. "All over the house, the closets, under beds, in the yard."

"I might know where she is. Check that little door." Seth pointed to the lower half of the built-in bookshelves separating the living room from the dining room.

Elise hurried across the room and opened the little door.

Olivia sat inside, grinning from ear to ear. "'Lise, found me. I hided."

Relief washing over her in a tidal wave of emotion, Elise

grabbed Olivia and pulled her out of the cubicle. Holding her tight, Elise sank to the floor and sobbed, releasing all her pent-up fear.

Olivia patted Elise's arm. "Why 'Lise crying?"

Elise held Olivia at arms' length. "I thought you were lost. Why didn't you answer when I called?"

"Playing hide-'n-seek like Daddy."

So that's how Seth knew where Olivia was hiding. "But you didn't tell me I was supposed to look for you. I didn't know you were playing a game."

"I told you."

But I wasn't listening. Her own thoughts convicted her. She'd been too busy cooking and thinking about Seth and hadn't paid enough attention to Olivia. While she'd been absorbed in her own thoughts, Olivia could have run out into the street and been hit by a car or walked away from the house and been snatched by some disturbed person. Elise took a deep breath as the horrible thoughts marched through her mind.

What must Seth be thinking? If something had happened to Olivia, how could she have faced him? How could she expect him to forgive her in those circumstances when she'd shown no forgiveness to him or Sophie?

Despite Sophie's mistake, she deserved to know her daughter. And Seth deserved the benefit of the doubt for making a mistake while dealing with a difficult and emotional decision. Elise knew she'd passed judgment while she was guilty of making mistakes in her own way.

"Daddy." Olivia jumped out of Elise's embrace and ran to Seth.

"Olivia, you scared Elise when you didn't answer her."

Gazing at Elise, Olivia scrunched up her little face. "I sorry, 'Lise."

"I'm the one who's sorry. I should've listened better." Elise's heart hammered as she scrambled to her feet. She wanted to fly into Seth's arms and tell him she'd been wrong not to talk things out with him, but instead, she gripped the back of the nearby chair. That was the problem she'd had all along. She'd tried to hide from her problems rather than talking about them.

"Is your grandfather going to be all right?"

"Yes." She had to make amends. As she stepped toward Seth, the smoke alarm in the kitchen began to blare. She turned toward the sound as a cloud of smoke and a burnt smell wafted into the living room. "Oh, no, I've burned the cookies."

Elise ran into the kitchen and retrieved the charred cookies from the oven. More smoke filled the room, and Seth opened the back door to let in some air.

Elise sank onto one of the kitchen chairs, then looked at Seth. "I've made a mess of everything. Especially us. You did the right thing for Olivia and Sophie."

Seth took one of Elise's hands and pulled her to her feet. "But I was wrong…wrong not to tell you about Sophie's letter from the very beginning. I should've talked to you and sought your advice. Forgive me."

Elise closed the gap between them and flung her arms around him. "Yes, and forgive me for not talking with you and working things out. I love you."

"I haven't ever stopped loving you." Seth held her tight. "So you're willing to work things out?"

Elise nodded, unable to speak.

"Willing to go with us on our first meeting with Sophie?"

Elise felt a tug on her pant leg. She looked down, and Olivia smiled up at her. Elise couldn't say no. Dealing with Sophie was part of learning to face her problems and not hide behind a wall of silence. If she loved Seth and Olivia, Elise knew she had to deal with Sophie's presence in their lives. "Yes."

Seth picked up his little girl. "What do you think, Olivia?"

Olivia clapped her little hands. "I loves Daddy. I loves 'Lise."

Seth pulled them both into his embrace. "Olivia has the right idea. We're going to love each other forever."

While Elise stood in the circle of Seth's arms with Olivia and drank in the wonder of this day, she realized God had answered her prayer. He'd shown her how to face her fears and be merciful, and in return she'd received mercy and love.

* * * * *

Dear Reader,

Thank you for choosing to read *Hometown Proposal*. I hope you enjoyed another story set in Kellerville. The journey that Elise and Seth took to reconciliation is a lesson in forgiveness and mercy. Sometimes forgiveness is hard because the hurt is so deep, but God can give us the strength to forgive and show mercy. When I don't feel very merciful, I like to remind myself of the story that Jesus told Matthew in 18:21-35.

I love to hear from readers. I enjoy your letters and e-mails so much. You can write to me at P.O. Box 16461, Fernandina Beach, Florida 32035, or through my Web site: www.merrilleewhren.com.

May God bless you,

Merrillee Whren

QUESTIONS FOR DISCUSSION

1. At the beginning of the story Elise is upset with her sister, Juliane, because she kept information about Seth a secret. Do you think Elise had justification for being upset? Has something like this happened to you? If so, how did you handle it?

2. Seth is worried about seeing Elise because he doesn't know how she will react to his having Olivia. How would you feel if you were in Elise's place?

3. The sudden death of Seth's father made him examine his life and make changes. Have you or someone you know had a tragic event precipitate a life-changing examination? Explain.

4. Although Elise doesn't want to be drawn into Seth's life, she feels the pressure from those around her to do the "right" thing when it comes to helping him. As Christians, we are often called to help those in need. Discuss the feelings that can accompany this call.

5. Elise thinks about how God wants her to treat Seth. How might the message in Luke 6:27-36 help her? Discuss the difficulties with following God's directives in these verses.

6. Seth is prompted by his faith to seek forgiveness from those he has hurt. Do you think asking for forgiveness can be as difficult as the forgiving? Why or why not?

7. Seth became a Christian, in part, because he saw how the church members gave his mother support when her husband died. Matthew 6:2-4 and John 13:35 are two scriptures that shed light on this subject. What do they say about how we should treat one another?

8. Both Elise and Seth have problems forgiving themselves for their past mistakes. Do you ever have problems forgiving yourself? How could these verses help? Psalm 103:11-13; Romans 4:7-8; 1 John 1:9

9. Seth wants desperately to reconcile with Elise, but he fears that God may have other plans for his life. How do the verses in Isaiah 55:8-9 relate to the lives of the characters in this story? How do they relate to your life?

10. Both Elise and Seth know that God has a plan for their lives, but often they are afraid to let God have complete control. Do you wonder about God's plan for your life? What do the following scriptures say about God's plans? Job 42:2; Proverbs 16:19; Proverbs 19:21; Jeremiah 28:11

11. Elise tells Seth that she believes God can use our lives even when we don't make a good decision. Do you agree with this statement? Why or why not?

12. Seth is haunted by the mistakes from his past. He fears that those mistakes will always be a barrier between Elise and him. Why do past wrongs often keep people apart? What can be done to prevent that from happening?

13. Father's Day creates mixed feelings for Seth. The day makes him remember his dad's death, but it also reminds

Seth what a blessing he has as Olivia's father. Holidays can be difficult times when we have lost loved ones. What steps can a person take to deal with those difficult times? What can a person do to remember the blessings?

14. Elise is hurt and confused by Sophie's reappearance in Seth's life. Do you think her reaction was reasonable? Why or why not? Have you or someone you know had to deal with a similar situation? If so, how did you handle it? How does the story of the unmerciful servant in Matthew 18:21-35 apply to the characters in this story?

Love Inspired®

TITLES AVAILABLE NEXT MONTH

Available August 31, 2010

BABY MAKES A MATCH
Chatam House
Arlene James

DOCTOR RIGHT
Alaskan Bride Rush
Janet Tronstad

SHELTER OF HOPE
New Friends Street
Lyn Cote

LOVE FINDS A HOME
Mirror Lake
Kathryn Springer

MADE TO ORDER FAMILY
Ruth Logan Herne

COURTING RUTH
Hannah's Daughters
Emma Miller

Enjoy a sneak peek at fan favorite Molly O'Keefe's
Harlequin Superromance miniseries,
THE NOTORIOUS O'NEILLS, *with*
TYLER O'NEILL'S REDEMPTION,
available September 2010
only from Harlequin Superromance.

Police chief Juliette Tremblant recognized the shape of the man strolling down the street—in as calm and leisurely fashion as if it were the middle of the day rather than midnight. She slowed her car, convinced her eyes were playing tricks on her. It had been a long time since Tyler O'Neill had been seen in this town.

As she pulled to a stop at the curb, he turned toward her, and her heart about stopped.

"What the hell are you doing here, Tyler?"

"Well, if it isn't Juliette Tremblant." He made his way over to her, then leaned down so he could look her in the eye. He was close enough to touch.

Juliette was not, repeat, *not* going to touch Tyler O'Neill. Not with her fingers. Not with a ten-foot pole. There would be no touching. Which was too bad, since it was the only way she was ever going to convince herself the man standing in front of her—as rumpled and heart-stoppingly handsome now as he'd been at sixteen—was real.

And not a figment of all her furious revenge dreams.

"What are you doing back in Bonne Terre?" she asked.

"The manor is sitting empty," Tyler said and shrugged, as though his arriving out of the blue after ten years was casual. "Seems like someone should be watching over the family home."

"You?" She laughed at the very notion of him being here for any unselfish reason. "Please."

He stared at her for a second, then smiled. Her heart fluttered against her chest—a small mechanical bird powered by that smile.

"You're right." But that cryptic comment was all he offered.

Juliette bit her lip against the other questions.

Why did you go?

Why didn't you write? Call?

What did I do?

But what would be the point? Ten years of silence were all the answer she really needed.

She had sworn off feeling anything for this man long ago. Yet one look at him and all the old hurt and rage resurfaced as though they'd been waiting for the chance. That made her mad.

She put the car in gear, determined not to waste another minute thinking about Tyler O'Neill. "Have a good night, Tyler," she said, liking all the cool "go screw yourself" she managed to fit into those words.

It seems Juliette has an old score to settle with Tyler.
Pick up TYLER O'NEILL'S REDEMPTION
to see how he makes it up to her.
Available September 2010,
only from Harlequin Superromance.

HARLEQUIN®

American ★ Romance®

TANYA MICHAELS
Texas Baby

Babies
&
Bachelors
USA

Instant parenthood is turning Addie Caine's life
upside down. Caring for her young nephew and
infant niece is rewarding—but exhausting! So when
a gorgeous man named Giff Baker starts a short-term
assignment at her office, Addie knows there's no time
for romance. Yet Giff seems to be in hot pursuit....
Is this part of his job, or can he really be falling
for her? And her chaotic, ready-made family!

**Available September 2010
wherever books are sold.**

"LOVE, HOME & HAPPINESS"

www.eHarlequin.com

HAR75325